Jubal pumped the action of the rifle and remained standing, staring across the intervening ground at the cluster of mounted braves in the mouth of the gorge. The Indians were motionless, hatred blazing in every pair of dark eyes. But there was something impotent about the braves, as if they were powerless to vent their fury without a triggering act to release it. But it wasn't that at all.

"Behind you!" Russ Longstreet screamed.

Jubal saw every brave's head swing, their anger draining under an onslaught of fear as they sought to identify a new enemy. Then he turned himself . . .

Danger and suspense wait around every bend as Jubal Cade battles the lethal arrows of the Sioux Indians and the treachery of the white man. Fighting his way west to avenge his wife's murder and help young Andy Prescott, Jubal must ultimately face THE DOUBLE CROSS.

Also by Charles R. Pike

THE KILLING TRAIL
THE HUNGRY GUN

Jubal Cade / 2

Double Cross

Charles R. Pike

CHELSEA HOUSE
New York, London
1980

Copyright © 1980 by Chelsea House Publishers, a division of
Chelsea House Educational Communications, Inc.
All rights reserved
First published in Great Britain in 1974 by Granada Publishing Limited
Printed and bound in the United States of America
LC: 80-68160
ISBN: 0-87754-231-7

Chelsea House Publishers
Harold Steinberg, Chairman & Publisher
Andrew E. Norman, President
Susan Lusk, Vice President

A Division of Chelsea House Educational Communications, Inc.
70 West 40 Street, New York 10018

CHAPTER ONE

'I hope you will agree that three hundred dollars a month is not excessive, Dr. Cade,' Professor Erich Lenz said, taking a large-faced watch from his vest pocket and checking the time. 'Now that you have seen the facilities I have here.'

Jubal Cade was aware that the bald-headed little German considered the interview at an end and awaited a decision. 'It's no bargain,' he replied as he turned his coat collar up against the bite of the winter air. 'But it's a fair price. It's the three months in advance that puts me in a bind.'

Lenz shrugged his broad shoulders. 'It is necessary as a sign of good faith. And as I explained earlier, it takes my staff and me at least three months to discover if we can help a child.'

Jubal nodded and looked across the frosted lawn to where the wagon was parked. Andy Prescott sat up on the box seat, his lithe body hunched against the cold, hands thrust deep into the pockets of his top coat. From a distance, it was impossible to see his face as more than a pale blur against the dark material of his coat and hat. But Jubal knew the face would be expressing the kind of deep sadness no ten-year-old boy should ever feel.

The wagon was parked at the top of the gravel driveway in front of the Lenz Clinic and College. It had done a lot of travelling – all the way from New England to St. Louis – and showed many signs of the hard, tragic trip. It looked particularly ill-used in its present surroundings. The combined clinic and college stood on the west bank of the Mississippi River to the south of the city: a very impressive building of brick rising to two storeys around three sides of a lush green lawn that ran down to a neat dock at the river's edge. That was at the rear of the property. At the front was a column-flanked entrance at the top of a flight of broad steps. Spread out before this were two more lawns, dotted with shade oaks, bisected by the driveway which ran down to wrought iron gates in a high brick wall. Through the gates was the road to St. Louis.

The building, its grounds and the boundary wall were as well cared for as the facilities of which their owner had spoken. For almost an hour, the fast-talking, self-assured Professor Lenz had been at pains to hide nothing from Jubal as they toured the building and then sat on one of the many wooden benches positioned beneath the leafless shade trees. Andy had accompanied the two men on the tour, holding on to Jubal's wrist and strolling forward confidently: with implicit faith that his guide would steer him clear of danger. Andy needed a guide because he was blind.

Not totally sightless: for the bullet which had entered his forehead did not touch the optic nerves. And Jubal had been fast in making use of his training as a surgeon to remove it before it could cause further damage. But the impact of the lead – perhaps the displacement of sensitive tissue or perhaps merely shock – had affected the boy's sight to the extent that now he could do no more than distinguish light from dark and discern movement within a few feet.

'I do not accept patient-pupils lightly, Dr. Cade,' Lenz said as he stood up from the bench and Jubal rose beside him. 'You saw the examination I gave the boy. I sincerely feel I can help him regain the sight in his right eye. The left, I don't know. Did I not feel this, I would tell you so.'

The man's expression was as earnest as his voice as he began to walk back towards the front of the building. Jubal fell in beside him and their shoes crunched on the frost-stiff grass.

'I believe that,' was all Jubal said in reply and there was silence between them until they reached the wagon.

There was nothing in Andy's bright blue eyes to betray his blindness. At first glance he looked like a reasonably healthy little boy. He had blond hair and the kind of near-pretty features that suggested adolescence would bring out the beginnings of masculine handsomeness. Despite the thick coat, it could be seen that he was thinner than he should be. But that was not to be wondered at by anyone who knew the degree of his suffering over recent weeks. The deprivations of the long trail from the east. Then the brutal loss of his parents and sister in the explosion of slaughter during which he was blinded. Finally, the horror of Mary Cade's violent death at a time when he was just beginning to regard Jubal and his bride as far more than adequate substitute parents.*

A youngster with less resilience and strength of character would have suffered far more than a loss of weight in such a vicious chain of circumstances.

'We going now, Jubal?' the boy asked eagerly, his expression doubtful.

Lenz had a round, almost cherubic face beneath his hairless dome. It glowed red with the cold, flawed by fewer age lines than a man of fifty-eight should have a right to expect. But he was obviously a man who, if he had ever found cause for concern, had been able to counteract anxiety from a vast storehouse of self-confidence. And this confidence in himself was based on a sound foundation: for Lenz was acknowledged to be the finest eye specialist in the world. As Jubal looked into the florid face, the German professor's self-assurance continued to be displayed in the form of calm indifference. He had enough patients already in his luxurious premises to keep the wolves far from the door. And as they left there would always be others waiting to step into the vacant places.

Jubal had been on the verge of anger since shortly after meeting Lenz and now the man's coldly take-it-or-leave-it attitude nudged him even closer to an outburst. But he struggled to check it, aware that to provoke the professor would inevitably destroy whatever chance Andy had of regaining his sight.

'Well, Dr. Cade?' Lenz posed, rubbing his hands together. Not avariciously. Just to combat the cold.

* See: *Jubal Cade: The Killing Trail.*

7

Andy had his head cocked on one side, sightless eyes seeming to pierce into the inside of Jubal's mind.

'We're leaving,' Jubal said curtly, and swung to look directly at Lenz. 'But only for so long as it takes me to raise the advance payment. We'll be back.'

Andy seemed to shrink even smaller inside his warm clothing. Lenz inclined his head as Jubal hauled himself up on to the wagon seat and unhitched the reins from around the brake lever.

'I'll look forward to seeing you and the boy,' the little German said evenly, but his small, dark eyes revealed he lacked conviction in the other man's determination. Then he turned and hurried up the steps. The front door of the impressive building was opened by an elderly man in a white medical smock. When it was closed the air seemed to become abruptly colder by several degrees.

'I ain't gonna like it there, Jubal,' Andy said as the four horse team responded to the slap of the reins across their backs, drawing the wagon into a turn to head down the driveway.

'Sure you will, Andy,' Jubal replied, injecting a lighter note into his voice. 'There are at least fifty other kids there, a lot of them your age or thereabouts.'

'I ain't never liked being with kids my own age,' Andy countered.

Jubal sighed. 'Do you want to be blind for the rest of your life, son?' he asked.

'Pa always said a man's gotta accept God's will,' Andy answered.

Despite his diminishing anger at Lenz and concern about how he was going to raise the nine hundred dollars, Jubal smiled. Andy's conversation was always liberally sprinkled with the proverbs and sayings picked up from his father.

'Didn't he always used to say that the Lord helps those who help themselves, Andy?'

Now the boy sighed, as Jubal steered the team out through the gateway and into a right hand turn towards the sprawl

8

of St. Louis. 'I used to notice how a lot of the things Pa said were kinda at odds with one another. But it don't matter, Jubal. I'd still rather help you find the guy that killed Mrs. Cade.'

Jubal felt his anger start to rise again. Not aimed at the boy. Instead, towards the tall gunslinger with a scar on his forehead who had pushed a Colt revolver into Mary's mouth and pulled the trigger. But again he struggled to contain the rage, knowing how futile was anger at this moment. And he succeeded by relegating the memory of Mary to the back of his mind. She was dead and buried and could suffer no further harm. And tracking down the man who killed her could wait. The boy was of immediate concern.

'He didn't think a lot of you, did he, Jubal?' Andy said after long moments had gone by.

It is nature's way to compensate the deprived and Jubal had witnessed this happening in the case of Andrew Prescott. The boy had lost his sight and almost at once had begun to develop an almost eerie new sense: one that enabled him to accurately assess the character of any stranger with whom he came into contact. It was almost as if he could read the minds without seeing the faces. But Jubal's medical training forced him to dismiss such an assumption and to rationalize the boy's newly acquired gift. Andy simply heard vocal tones and nuances more clearly than sighted people and was more sensitive to the subtle atmosphere that was generated in all social contact.

Jubal forced a laugh and knew that Andy recognized it for what it was – a hollow mask trying to hide anxiety. 'I don't exactly look like a man able to raise nine hundred dollars by snapping his fingers,' he said.

Which was right, for Jubal's appearance was as wearily travel-scarred as that of the wagon. His clothes had once been of the kind a young English doctor might be expected to wear. They had, in fact, been purchased in London at the conclusion of Jubal's seven-year medical studies in England. A black top coat, fur-lined and reaching to just above the

9

knees, worn over a grey suit and matching vest: with a white shirt, black bootlace necktie, black patent leather shoes and grey derby to complete the picture of sartorial elegance. But time and the miles of travel had taken their toll. First on the long boat trip across the Atlantic Ocean, bringing his English bride to his native land. Then over almost half the continent. Dirt and sweat, dust and blood, filth and tears were now ingrained in the expensive materials. Smart creases had long since disappeared and worn patches showed in many places.

And just as the clothes showed the unmistakable signs of misuse and neglect, so too did the man who wore them. He was not a big man: just topping five feet six inches. But he was well built with a large-boned frame cloaked with solid flesh. Thus he appeared slim without frailness, his body and the way he held it suggesting compact power. It was in his face that the strain of the recent past was clearly visible. The features seemed to hint at callow youthfulness on first glance and at the time he stepped ashore at New York Harbour it would have been difficult to see through this to the depths of Jubal's strength of character. Now it was easy, for the pain and anguish he had suffered was inscribed upon every plane and hollow: visible in the lines etched deeply into the taut skin turned dark brown by exposure to the elements. It was a lean face, dominated by deep-set brown eyes that had lost the ability to smile and constantly searched their surroundings for a sign of danger. Beneath the eyes the cheek bones were high and prominent, seeming to pull the skin up from the firm jawline which in turn dragged it down. His mouth was full and this did smile easily, the lips cracking to display two broken teeth which were inclined to continue the boyishness which he had so recently possessed. But when Jubal smiled, his brow beneath his black, close-cropped hair crinkled and this emphasized the sheen on the scar tissue at the bridge of his nose. And the shattered teeth and dead skin became the blatant signs of physical suffering which could only be guessed at from the cold light in the dark eyes.

But a man had to look long at Jubal to detect that he was not as he had always been. And Erich Lenz was too wrapped up in his own contentment to examine the man in depth. He had simply seen the dishevelled clothes, dirt-grimed hands and heavily stubbled jowls and jaw. From these obvious signs of neglect he had judged his visitor to be just another anxious parent hopeful of trading on sympathy without the need for money to change hands.

'But you're gonna raise it, ain't you, Jubal,' Andy said sadly.

'Sure am,' Jubal replied resolutely, and he could not recall when he had last felt so determined about anything. He draped an arm around the boy's shoulder. 'And not only because I think he can do your eyes some good, Andy.'

The boy was confused. 'What else?' he wanted to know.

Jubal laughed and this time there was a ring of genuine humour in the sound. 'It's a school as well as a clinic,' he reminded the boy. 'And while Lenz is fixing your eyes a teacher will be fixing the way you talk. Who knows, you might even learn not to say *ain't* and *gonna* all the time.'

'School!' Andy exclaimed distastefully.

Jubal tightened his arm around the boy. 'You want to be stupid all your life?' he asked lightly.

But the boy refused to respond to Jubal's attempt at brightening the mood. He thrust his hands deeper into his pockets and closed his vacant eyes. His body was held rigid and swayed stiffly with the motion of the wagon rolling along the rutted road.

Jubal decided to let the boy think about the proposition for a while and took the reins in both hands again, clucking to the team for more speed towards the city. St. Louis was an unattractive dark smudge on the bright afternoon. Overhead the winter sky was clear of cloud and the sun shed an angry glare, as if enraged that it could not generate enough heat to melt the frost coating the earth. The frost crystals glinted in response. Ice floes moving sluggishly downstream in the broad Mississippi also caught the rays of the ineffectual sun and flashed in reply. But all this was out in open country:

11

rolling prairie split by the river and featured with stands of timber and the occasional neat farmsteads to the west of the road from the Lenz property to the city. The city itself neither accepted nor refracted the shafting sunlight. Or at least it did not seem to do so from a distance. For above it hovered a gigantic pall of black smoke from countless chimneys: as if St. Louis was sulking beneath a cloud of depression.

It would have been easy for Jubal to see the view as a manifestation of his own mood, but he shook free of the temptation. He had gone out to see Professor Lenz expecting no more than he received. In a way, the trip had produced more than he had hoped for. In two ways, he corrected himself. First, the little German's obvious low opinion of him as a potential client had hardened Jubal's determination to obtain for Andy the best attention money could buy. And secondly, the clinic had proved to be everything he had heard about it. In short, it offered exactly what Jubal had in mind for Andy, and nothing was going to stand in the way of the boy's being sent there.

'Does St. Louis look as ugly from this side as you said it did from across the river?' Andy asked to end his long period of introspection.

'Worse, if anything,' Jubal answered.

'So I reckon we oughta move on,' the boy suggested in a tone that revealed he already knew the kind of response he would draw.

'No chance, son,' Jubal told him, gazing along the road. 'People live in cities because there's money in them. And money is what we need right now.'

'Money to leave me here so you can move on,' Andy accused. 'I'm from the country.'

The boy was not a whiner. When he complained it was in a doleful tone that made a request rather than a demand.

'Make a deal with you,' Jubal said.

'What kinda deal?' Andy asked, half-interested.

'Moment you can see just how ugly a city is, I'll come and get you.'

'That ain't no deal if I can't get cured, Jubal,' Andy replied immediately.

Jubal was on the point of telling him not to think in such a negative way, but held back. Lenz was good, but not a miracle worker and it would be bad for the boy if all doubt was erased. 'All right, son. If it turns out that way, I'll let you come with me the day you can talk for five minutes without saying ain't.'

'Easy,' Andy boasted.

'Yeah?'

'Ain't no trouble at all.'

Andy swallowed hard and Jubal laughed. Andy looked crestfallen for a few moments, then burst into laughter himself. As the wagon rolled through the southern fringes of the city Jubal realized this was the first time the boy had been happy since they left to go out to the clinic.

St. Louis was bustling at its commercial centre, the streets thick with traffic and the sidewalks crowded. Vehicles and pedestrians were all in a hurry, obviously to get somewhere but apparently going nowhere. Jubal had been brought up in a Chicago orphanage and also knew New York and London. But despite this metropolitan background he had never been able to come to terms with the hustle and bustle of city life. He was certain his parents had been country folk.

The hotel into which he had checked the previous night was the Adams, on the corner of Broadway and Washington Avenue. It was a rundown three-storey frame firetrap smelling of damp and the cheap perfume of the whores who operated out of the first floor rooms. Not the kind of place where he would have chosen to take a ten-year-old boy; even one unable to see his surroundings. But after crossing the Mississippi it was the first hotel they had come to which appeared to be within his strict budget. And the slovenly desk clerk had raised no objection to accepting a guest of such tender years: once he had received payment in advance from Jubal.

A livery stable on St. Charles Street took in the wagon and team for a second night and Jubal led Andy along Broadway to the hotel. It was too early for any of the whores to be on show in the sagging easy chairs of the rancid-smelling lobby. But the middle-aged, almost toothless clerk looked up avariciously at the sound of the opening door. Disappointment spread across his blotched face as he recognized Jubal. Then, unaccountably, a frown of guilt twisted his features.

'No messages, Mr. Cade,' he said quickly as Jubal looked at him.

'Pity,' Jubal said, leading Andy across the moth-eaten carpet towards the foot of the stairway.

The clerk was surprised. 'You expecting something?'

'Hoping,' Jubal replied. 'For someone to leave me a thousand dollars.'

The clerk swallowed hard. 'You gotta be kidding.'

'If I asked someone to leave it with you I'd have to be crazy,' Jubal called back as he started up the stairway.

He looked back over his shoulder and saw that the clerk was looking guilty again. The man's attitude worried him and he moved faster up the stairway, along the hallway and up the next flight to the third floor. He had grown adept at leading his blind charge and Andy had become accustomed to trusting his guide.

'We got some trouble, Jubal?' the boy asked.

'Maybe,' Jubal replied as he stopped outside the room door and dug for his key.

The door was locked and on the other side the room appeared precisely as he had left it before going out to see Professor Lenz. The distant view of St. Louis crouched under a thick cloud had been an optical illusion. The cold glare of the sun easily penetrated the smoke pall and enough of its light filtered in through the dirt-grimed window to show up every part of the small, spartanly furnished room. Andy found his own way to one of the two single beds and sat down on the edge of it while Jubal went to the clothes closet and bureau standing at right angles to each other in a corner. The bureau was empty of anything belonging to Jubal and the boy, but in the closet was a Spencer rifle and a

14

small black valise containing medical supplies and surgical instruments. The rifle appeared to have been untouched since Jubal stored it in the corner. But he was certain the valise had been moved.

'Something wrong?' the boy asked as Jubal took out the valise and rested it on the bed.

'Maybe.' He opened the valise and bared his teeth in a silent snarl. A half-pint bottle of pure alcohol was missing. 'Change that to yes,' he told Andy as he closed up the valise and replaced it in the closet. 'Stay put, son. I have to go downstairs.'

As Jubal went to the door, Andy seemed on the point of saying something. But he remained silent, sensing his un-official guardian was angry and not wishing to get caught in a backlash.

Jubal went down the two flights of stairs slowly, struggling to contain his rage. He was a fully trained physician and surgeon, dedicated to saving life. It was therefore reasonable for him to detest the theft of one of his tools. But he also knew himself to be a killer, capable of taking life in a fit of anger.

When he reached the lobby he was still boiling inside, but thought he had the rage in check. He caught a glimpse of himself in a mottled mirror and his face appeared calm. The skin was no tighter than usual over his features, his eyes were cold and his mouth was not compressed.

Two whores, slumped wearily on a sagging sofa, eyed him professionally for a moment, then lost interest when they saw he was intent upon the desk clerk. The blotched face of the near toothless man looked more guilty than ever as he met the steady gaze of Jubal. Then fear contorted the features as Jubal halted immediately in front of the desk and slowly unbuttoned his top coat.

'Want to report a theft from my room,' Jubal announced flatly.

The whores were abruptly interested in him again. They

15

were still young but life had been bad to them and their weary eyes counteracted whatever attractiveness they might have possessed.

The clerk swallowed hard. 'Management ain't responsible for valuables left in the rooms,' he bleated.

Jubal leaned across the desk and the clerk tried to step backwards. But Jubal's arm streaked out and his hand bunched the man's shirt front. As he jerked the clerk towards him, the man caught his breath. 'Say that again!' His tone was still flat.

'The management —'

Jubal grimaced at the stink of the man's breath. 'That's enough,' he said. 'You got a pass key to the rooms and you smell like a still.'

He stepped back abruptly, retaining his grip of the shirt front. The clerk gave a cry of alarm as he was lifted from the floor and dragged across the desk. Jubal continued to move back until the clerk slammed down on to his feet again in front of the desk.

'Hell, mister. I only had but a couple of slugs.' The saliva of fear welled up in his mouth and spilled from a corner to run down his grizzled chin.

The whores watched avidly, starved of excitement and determined to get their fill at this opportunity.

'Just two?' Jubal asked, holding the man out at arm's length.

The clerk was trembling, his hands clenching and unclenching. But he made no move to raise his arms in defence of himself. His watery eyes were trapped again by Jubal's impassive gaze and he blinked rapidly, several times. He opened his mouth to speak, then changed what he had intended to say. 'Maybe a couple more,' he admitted. 'Almost half the bottle left.' More saliva spilled. 'I'll pay you. Name your price.'

'Nine hundred dollars,' Jubal replied.

More rapid blinking. 'You must be crazy!' the clerk accused.

16

'Mad, maybe,' Jubal told him. Abruptly, he jerked the clerk towards him. The clerk brought up his arms now, but Jubal used his knee. As he slammed the man's body against his own, he snapped up his leg. The kneecap smashed into the man's crotch and a high-pitched wail burst from his mouth. The strength drained from his legs and it was only Jubal's grip that held him upright. As the man reached down towards the source of the pain, Jubal shot his arm forward again. The clerk was slammed back against the front of the desk. His legs were still useless and he slumped down hard. He continued to wail and to clutch at himself, rolling on to his side and folding his body almost double.

There was a flap in the top of the desk at one end and Jubal raised it to pass through. Under the centre of the desk were two shelves and the bottle of raw alcohol stood on the top one, uncorked and within easy reach. It was less than a quarter full. He looked up to find the two whores eyeing him apprehensively.

'Two plus a couple more,' he said, holding up the bottle as he returned to the front of the desk. 'He's got a big mouth.'

The sounds of the clerk's pain had receded in pitch to a series of low groans intermingled with sighs.

The redheaded whore laughed harshly. 'Bet he's small someplace else, mister.'

'Bitch!' the clerk rasped.

Jubal crossed the lobby and started up the stairs as the whores rose and stood over the groaning clerk.

'You want us to make you a big man again, Luke?' the bleached blonde asked with derisive gentleness.

'Only a dollar each, Luke,' the redhead added.

Luke glared up at the whores and opened his mouth to yell at them. But the pain combined with the raw alcohol in his stomach to well nausea into his throat. Stinking vomit spewed from his mouth. Both whores leapt back in revulsion from the flood.

'Guess that means he ain't interested,' the blonde said,

swinging around to look up at Jubal ascending the stairway. 'How about you, mister?'

Jubal showed his broken-toothed grin. 'Luke said it for me, too,' he answered and turned away from the vicious snarls on the whores' faces.

CHAPTER TWO

Jubal knew that the mere fact of staying at the Adams Hotel was bad for an impressionable ten-year-old boy. To leave Andy alone in the place was unthinkable. Which meant he had to lead the youngster through the night-time street of St. Louis, a city overflowing with the suppliers of and customers for every kind of human degeneration.

When he guided Andy out of the hotel after nightfall, under the curious and rather apprehensive eye of a new, older desk clerk, Jubal no longer looked as if he belonged in such a place. He had taken a bath and shaved. And sponged off all but the most ingrained stains from his clothes. He had also put the protesting Andy in the tub and then done what he could to clean up the boy's shirt, levis and top coat.

A clock was striking ten as they emerged on to Washington Avenue and Andy had to stifle a yawn before he could ask the question which he had phrased in at least a dozen different ways since Jubal had announced they were going out. 'You ready to tell me now where we're going?'

Jubal looked up the avenue, then moved a few paces south to survey Broadway in both directions. 'Make some money,' he answered, leading the boy north on Washington, towards a cluster of lights some three blocks away.

'Just like that?' Andy asked dully.

'Won't be easy,' Jubal agreed, ignoring the curious stares from some of the passers-by.

'I reckon it's impossible,' Andy replied. 'Nobody can make nine hundred dollars in one night.'

'Already got three hundred and fifty,' Jubal told his young charge. 'And I don't figure to spend the whole night making it up.'

Among the buildings lining both sides of the avenue in the

brightly lit area he saw two theatres, several bars and a couple of hotels.

'Jubal?'

'Yes, son?'

'You ain't gonna do anything against the law, are you, Jubal?'

Jubal tightened his grip on the boy's hand. 'You really think I would, Andy?' he asked. He halted to look down at the boy and Andy flushed and shook his head. Jubal laughed. 'Not unless they made playing poker a crime.'

They began to walk again and Jubal had to be more careful in leading the boy through the heavy press of people on the sidewalk under the bright lights. Men were laughing and women were shrieking. Music and singing spilled out through many doorways. Andy had to shout to make himself heard above the raucous din.

'Pa always said gambling was a sin!'

'Not gambling, son,' Jubal called back absently as he looked at the façades of two large hotels across the avenue. 'Just gambling and losing.'

The hotels were nothing like the Adams. They were brick built, springing up six storeys, dripping with light from sparklingly clean windows. Each had an awning over the impressive entrance, attended by a uniformed doorman. A constant stream of cabs angled into the sidewalk to deposit well-dressed ladies and their escorts in front of the hotels. Because of the amount of traffic on the avenue, Jubal lifted Andy and carried him over to the other side. When he set him down again on the opposite sidewalk, Andy dusted himself off disdainfully.

'I don't like to be carried,' he complained.

'Rather get run down by a buggy and pair?' Jubal asked lightly against the background noise of genteel dance music coming from the entrance of the St. Louis City Hotel.

'Might be better than staying at that clinic place,' Andy replied as he was led towards the arched entrance of the St. Charles House.

'Don't be a grouch,' Jubal told the boy good-humouredly. 'Or I may make you stay there until you can see *and* learn not to say *ain't*.'

'Can I help you, sir?' the doorman of the St. Charles House asked as Jubal guided Andy towards the entrance.

He was a big man, bulging out his white uniform with the shined buttons and gold shoulder tabs. He stepped smoothly into Jubal's path.

'You got five hundred and fifty dollars?' Jubal asked.

The doorman had been eyeing Jubal's style and condition of dress with undisguised contempt. Now he showed anger. 'Get lost.'

'No, you can't help me,' Jubal told him flatly. 'So get out of the way and let us in.'

The doorman bristled as he looked down at Jubal, over a head smaller. 'Why you —' A carriage drew to a halt at the sidewalk and the driver shouted. The doorman's lower lip quivered. 'So you're gonna get in, punk,' he rasped as he moved towards the waiting guests. 'But I'll be here when you come out.'

'Luck runs my way you'll be able to get us a cab,' Jubal called after him as he led Andy up the three white steps and through the swing doors into the lobby.

It was palatial. Marble walls, thick carpet scattered with deep armchairs and sofas, a flying staircase, crystal chandeliers and luxuriously warm air heavy with the scent of expensive perfume and high-priced cigars.

'Smells rich, Jubal,' Andy said softly.

People stood or sat in groups. Others moved into and out of arched doorways with wrought iron signs above them: *Restaurant, Bar, Billiards Room, Smoking Room*. The men were mostly in evening dress, the women in ornate gowns. Jewellery flashed and high-toned conversation hummed. As at the Lenz clinic, Jubal was self-conscious about his appearance.

'Pretty ritzy,' he informed the boy, starting across the thick pile carpet towards the archway marked as the entrance to the smoking room. Most of the people in the lobby were too wrapped up in their companions to notice the man and boy. But a few cast quizzical glances in their direction. Jubal noted some hurried activity at the curved reception desk and spotted, without appearing to, the despatch of a grey-haired, round-shouldered man of early middle age. The man had to weave this way and that to avoid breaking through groups, but maintained an ultimate course which brought him to the smoking room entrance just ahead of Jubal and Andy.

The man wore a tuxedo and black tie. The starched collar of his white shirt seemed uncomfortable and his thick neck was red from chafing. He was the same height as Jubal, but broader. His dark eyes had a dangerous glint in them. A fat cigar was gripped in two fingers of a many-ringed hand and he blew smoke at Jubal as the two men halted.

'No children allowed in the smoke room,' he said, trying to sound refined but not making it.

Jubal nodded. 'Hoping you'd have a rule about that. This little guy's getting to be a grouch and he might cramp my style.'

'Gee, Jubal,' Andy said.

'Boy that age ought to be at home in bed,' the man criticized.

'House detective?' Jubal guessed.

'Right.'

Jubal leaned to the side to look around the detective. Some of the men through the archway were smoking. But merely as an ancillary pursuit. There were a dozen of them, split into three groups of four at green baize-covered tables. Poker was the game in every case, played in bright pools of light that left the remainder of the large room in murky darkness.

'That's good,' Jubal told the man as he straightened up. 'Means your job is to see the patrons and their property come to no harm. Take care of Andy for me, will you? If you can snap him out of his misery he's not such a bad kid.'

'Jubal!' Andy yelled as the detective looked from the man to the boy and back again in open-mouthed surprise.

Jubal released the small hand and dropped an arm over the narrow shoulders. Then he crouched down beside the boy and made his voice earnestly tender. 'Look, Andy, you know the

22

spot we're in,' he said, aware that the shout had attracted the attention of many of the people in the lobby. 'Didn't your Pa ever say something about needs must when the devil drives?'

Andy's lower lip trembled and he bit it. His tired eyes were misted by the threat of tears. There was a quiver in his voice. 'You won't be long, Jubal?'

Jubal placed both his hands on the boy's shoulders and gave them a reassuring squeeze. 'Old Lady Luck takes her own time, son. But I'll do what I can to hurry her along.'

The buzz of conversation rose to its former level again as people lost interest in the scene outside the smoking room. But an itch at the nape of his neck told Jubal that at least one pair of eyes was still trained intently upon him.

'I ain't no baby-minder!' the house detective snarled softly, dropping all pretence at refinement.

'I ain't no baby neither!' Andy retorted, drawing his frail body to its full height.

'Pardon me,' a woman said diffidently as Jubal rose.

As he turned towards the newcomer, the detective took the opportunity to move swiftly away. She was in her late thirties, perhaps early forties, and still retained traces of a once fragile beauty. A tall and slim blonde, she had a finely chiselled face from which her eyes looked out as if in constant horror at what they saw. Her dress was so plain that it had to be expensive to wear in such surroundings. It was cut low to expose the upper swells of small breasts. From around her neck, her wrists and the fingers of both hands diamonds glinted in gold settings. Jubal guessed the woman was wearing five times the money he hoped to raise in the smoking room.

He took off his derby as Andy moved in close to him and hooked an arm around his legs. 'Ma'am?'

She flashed a smile and then hid it as if she were ashamed of it. 'Forgive me. I couldn't help overhearing just now.' She held a small purse and kept digging her long-nailed fingers into it as she looked down at Andy. 'Ladies are like children,' she went on addressing the boy now. 'We aren't allowed in the smoking room either.' Her eyes flicked up to Jubal's face

23

again. 'My husband is inside. If you must go in there, I'll be happy to look after the boy.'

Andy tightened his arm around Jubal's leg and when Jubal glanced down at him he was surprised to find the boy looking more apprehensive than ever. When he returned his gaze to the woman, she was wearing another smile. This one was longer lived, but held a deep sadness.

'I realize he is blind,' she said. 'I saw from the way you guided him.'

'That's kind of you, ma'am,' Jubal said. He looked down. 'How about staying with the lady, Andy? You can tell her why I'm doing this so she won't think so badly of me.'

'I'd rather stay with you,' Andy replied, chewing on his lower lip again and seeming to stare hard at the woman. Then he sighed and transferred his sightless gaze up into the face of Jubal. 'But I won't be a grouch no more, so I'll stay with her if that's what you want.'

'Her name is Mrs. Gloria Agnew,' the woman said, her voice and smile suddenly a great deal brighter. She thrust out a hand towards Andy. 'Shall we go and sit down, young man?'

Jubal extricated himself from the boy's arm and guided his hand into that of Mrs. Agnew. 'I appreciate it, ma'am,' he said.

She waved away thanks, giving the impression that it was she who should be grateful. 'My husband is the man in the purple dinner jacket,' she explained. 'So you'll know when he leaves and I'll have to go.'

She tugged gently at the boy's hand and Andy trailed in her wake towards a vacant sofa. Jubal watched until they were both seated, then turned to enter the smoking room: confident that if the husband of such a jewel-bedecked woman was playing, the game was not penny-ante. The atmosphere within the room was permeated only by the masculine odours of nervous sweat and cigar smoke. Although there was no door in the archway, the room was noticeably quieter than the lobby. Conversation was curt and muted, confined to the minimum necessary to play poker. Heavy breathing and the occasional protest of a chair provided background noise. There was no clink of coinage, for it was not that kind of game.

From the threshhold, Jubal spotted the purple-jacketed Agnew playing in the game at the centre of the three tables. He surveyed the rest of the room, beyond the cones of lights and saw it was empty. No men waiting to join a game or start a new one. He did not advance, but stayed silhouetted in the archway as he lit a cheroot and drew against it contentedly. It was fifteen minutes before the game at each table ended simultaneously.

'Any of you gentlemen needs to take a break, be happy to sit in,' he announced.

A dozen heads were turned towards him. All were well-groomed, middle-aged to elderly. All had to be rich, for in the period he had been watching, Jubal had seen at least ten thousand dollars move back and forth across the tables.

'Unless there's a rule about not playing with strangers,' Jubal added after he had been examined in silence for long seconds.

'It's the money that don't have to be strange,' a man said, and several others laughed.

'You can take this chair, mister,' a tall, snow-haired old man said miserably, pushing back from the table at which Agnew sat. 'If you don't mind following a loser.'

He took the jacket off the back of the chair and shrugged into it as Jubal approached the table and looked at the three remaining players in turn.

'Welcome,' Agnew said.

'Fine with me,' the dealer acknowledged.

'Sit yourself down, son,' invited the third man.

Jubal nodded and took off his top coat, which he folded and placed on an empty table nearby before taking the vacant seat. Everyone in the room called goodnight to the departing player.

'Game is five card draw with dealer calling the wild cards,' Agnew explained. 'Aces are high and the stakes can be if you've a mind.'

Jubal was aware that he was being closely studied by his fellow players as the other two games got under way again. He didn't object, for he treated the three men to an equally fine examination. Because he had met the man's wife, he paid particular attention to Agnew. He was about forty-five, tall but running to fat to the extent that it showed. He had thinning black hair pasted down by grease. His face was round and fleshy, floridly unhealthy. His eyes seemed weak. His bankroll was strong. Biggest on the table.

'Agnew,' he said and nodded to the dealer. 'Bedlow.' A stubby finger indicated the third man. 'Gilman.'

'Cade,' Jubal responded.

'We don't take no markers,' Bedlow said pointedly, thrusting the deck towards Agnew for a cut.

As the cut was made, Jubal carefully drew the three hundred and fifty dollars from the inside pocket of his jacket. There was a fifty on top and the remainder were a mixture of ten, fives and ones. A lot of ones, because it was a thick stack.

'Run 'em,' Agnew said.

'Deuces made high,' Bedlow said. 'I'm making them wild.'

He dealt, anti-clockwise, each player getting a card in turn. Nothing fancy. Gilman opened and Jubal stayed for the sake of five dollars to try to improve on a pair of tens. Nothing, so he folded. Bedlow won a pot worth seventy-five dollars. Jubal lost fifteen dollars in the next hand. Agnew won the pot. Jubal dealt himself three of a kind with a wild queen and won two hundred dollars by drawing a pair for a full house. It worried him, winning for the first time on his own deal for he knew he was being tested, watched, assessed. But the deadpan attitudes of the other players did not alter.

Now that he was at a table, under the cone of light from the ceiling lamp, he was not aware at all of the muted noise from the hotel lobby. He did not even hear the voices of the men engaged in the other two games. The deal went around the table once more and, like the other men, Jubal both won and lost small amounts. But he was four hundred and fifty dollars ahead when Agnew pushed back his chair.

'Goin'?' Bedlow asked.

'Not on your life,' Agnew replied. 'I have to take a leak. And check Gloria's okay.'

Jubal was on the point of mentioning his meeting with Mrs. Agnew, but the man moved away from the table quickly. Bedlow filled the lull by prodding at his teeth with an ivory pick. Gilman rose and moved about the room, stretching his legs. Jubal lit a cheroot from the stub of the old and checked his pocket watch. The game was thirty minutes old as far as he was concerned. Without a hand of cards he had time to worry about the boy. Andy would be feeling low, each passing minute seeming to last an hour in his dark world. But while conscious of the boy's distress, Jubal did not try to think himself into a mood for making a rash plunge. He had learned the rudiments of poker at the Chicago foundlings' home and become an expert during medical training. And from almost the first game he had played seriously the cardinal rule had been detachment. In poker all that mattered were the fifty-two cards and the other players. For a man's mind to be concerned with anything outside this ... such a man was either a fool or did not care if he lost.

'Right, gentleman. Let's get back to business.'

Agnew had bustled back into the smoking room, his pudgy hands and bloated face rinsed clean of sweat. He sat down and merely glanced fleetingly at Jubal.

'Your wife okay, sir?' Jubal asked.

'Got the kind of male company I don't mind her having,' Agnew replied as Gilman resumed his seat. 'Boy's happy enough, Cade. Who's to deal?'

The first hand after the break was a pass and the second one produced another seventy-five dollars towards the total Jubal aimed at. He now had eight hundred and seventy-five dollars and knew he had reached the danger point of a game in which he had set himself a target. Nine hundred even would pay Lenz's fee but leave Jubal flat broke. But would he be able to call a halt after making the next twenty-five plus whatever bonus happened to be in the pot?

27

Agnew dealt the cards in the usual silence. Jubal picked up his hand in a neat pile and fanned them. Queen of hearts, seven of hearts, queen of clubs and eight and nine of hearts. Gilman opened for twenty-five, Jubal and Agnew stayed and Bedlow folded. Gilman drew three cards. Jubal made a snap decision and threw away the odd queen to draw one, knowing the odds were stacked high against him. He had been playing poker for many years, so his expression did not alter an iota when he made the king flush. Agnew drew three cards.

Chair legs scraped against the floor and there was conversation at another table as the game broke up. The sounds had an unreal quality. Bedlow began to pick at his teeth again.

'Let's start at fifty,' Gilman said.

'Stay,' Jubal followed, pushing a single note into the centre of the table.

Agnew considered a moment, staring at his cards and taking a deep breath. Then he smiled. 'Sort out the men from the boys,' he said, counting some bills off his pile. 'Fifty and up two-fifty, gentlemen.'

'Too rich for me and what I got,' Gilman muttered, disenchanted, as he folded his hand.

Jubal considered, running the mental arithmetic through his mind. There was four hundred and seventy-five dollars in the pot of which only seventy-five was his. It would cost him two-fifty to see Agnew and if he won he would be three-fifty ahead of his target. The odds in favour of him winning were enormous. For he could only be beaten by a better king flush, an ace flush, a running or a royal flush. All hard to come by, especially since Agnew had called no wild cards.

But if he raised? Jubal was faced by the inevitable problem of a man with a limited budget sitting in on a high stakes game. Agnew had only to raise again – by an amount greater than Jubal had in front of him.

'I'm calling you, Mr. Agnew,' Jubal said softly, pushing two-fifty into the pot.

He sensed his opponent's level stare upon him, but concentrated upon the five cards which Agnew spread on the table.

'Wise decision, son,' the man in the purple jacket said without condescension.

The cards showed a run in spades from the five to the nine. Jubal tossed his hand on to the discards of Gilman and Bedlow, his action and expression calm. When he looked up at Agnew's face, the man was showing no more than the expected amount of satisfaction at winning what for him was a small pot.

'Reckon that's me done for tonight, gentlemen,' he said, stretching and yawning.

Jubal looked hurriedly at Gilman and Bedlow and found them nodding in agreement.

'Don't like to keep my little lady waiting too long for dinner,' Agnew added, eyeing Jubal levelly. 'Guess you can't complain, son. You're ahead, aren't you?'

Jubal nodded, knowing exactly by how much. He had upped his starting money from three-fifty to five-fifty. 'No complaints, sir,' he said as Gilman and Bedlow rose and made their farewells.

Jubal glanced at the next table where a game was still in progress, the players down to their shirt sleeves and sitting amid a thick cloud of cigar smoke. The pot was a minor mountain of money.

'No chance, son,' Agnew said softly, with a note of mild sympathy in his voice. 'That session won't end until morning. And they never let in strangers.'

Jubal swung his head around to look again at Agnew, sensing the man had laid the first step towards making a point. The weak eyes were dark pools of understanding in the depths of their sockets.

'The boy told my wife about your problem, son,' Agnew said. 'But I'm kinda glad I had the beating of you in that last hand.'

The game was over and with it the tension of winning and losing had past. But the subject Agnew had raised caused the sounds from the next table and those from the hotel lobby to retreat further than ever.

'You want me to ask why?' Jubal said tensely.

'You want me to say it's none of my business?' Agnew countered coldly.

Jubal began to gather up his money and Agnew followed suit. 'No harm in you talking and me listening.'

Agnew nodded and sighed. 'If you'd won that game, son, could be you'd have decided that poker was the way out of your problem entirely. Three hundred bucks is a lot of scratch to find every month. And that only pays the German sawbones. You have to live, too.'

'Andy talks a lot,' Jubal said.

'Gambling ought to be a pleasure, son,' Agnew went on. 'Sure, some fellers make a living at it. But it's a mighty precarious living. Man with your responsibilities needs something a little more stable, I'd say.'

'Losing one hand wouldn't have changed my mind, if I was considering it,' Jubal replied.

Agnew smiled. 'Glad you feel that way, son. Otherwise you might have felt I rigged that last hand to make you more amenable to my proposition.'

Jubal kept his expression casual. 'Still no harm in my listening,' he said in response to Agnew's quizzical look.

Agnew drew in a deep breath. 'I'll pay you five thousand dollars to ride to Cheyenne and back, son,' he said softly.

The invisible wall of tension now blotted out every other sound in the hotel so that Jubal's voice was like a shout in the wilderness. But first he did the sum, producing the answer that the money would pay for something over sixteen months of treatment at the clinic. 'How many people do I have to kill on the way?' he asked.

Agnew's reply was a tiny scratch on the vast silence of the same wilderness. 'Up to you, son. Many as you like, so long as you deliver the package I give you.'

Reality returned and the smoking room was once more invaded by sound from the lobby, punctuated by the staccato raises and calls at the next table. Beyond the cone of light, Jubal saw two figures silhouetted in the archway. The woman holding the hand of the child.

'What will be in the package, Mr. Agnew?' he asked.

The elder man leaned across the table to whisper: 'One hundred thousand dollars.'

'I see,' Jubal replied.

'With five thousand dollars going for him, so might the kid,' Agnew pointed out.

Jubal showed his broken toothed grin. 'Looks like the eyes have it,' he said.

CHAPTER THREE

'Come back soon, Jubal,' Andy Prescott called from the stoop of the house.

Jubal swung up into the saddle of the chestnut stallion Ben Agnew had loaned him and looked across at the boy. 'I won't waste any time, son,' he replied.

Andy stood between the Agnews, wan-faced and looking more frail than ever since taking off the warm top coat. He looked cold. So did the couple flanking him. But behind them the open door of the house extended a bright welcome to the warmth offered inside. Jubal and Andy had shared a meal with the Agnews at the hotel and over the dinner table the details of the deal had been discussed: Andy listening in blank-faced silence. Then they had all left the city in Agnew's plush carriage, going by way of the Adams Hotel for Jubal to collect his valise and gun and the St. Charles Street livery to arrange long-time care of the team and storage of the wagon.

The Agnews' house was a single-storey, very spacious frame building a mile west of St. Louis on the Jefferson City turnpike. Spread northwards at the back of the house were many square miles of wheat and beef land from which Agnew had made his money: a great deal of money, that was obvious.

There had been no opportunity for Jubal and Andy to speak together privately at the hotel or on the trip out. And at the house Gloria Agnew took the boy to his room while Jubal was invited to pick out a horse and equipment from the stable. Ben Agnew disappeared into his study for some time and then brought out a bulky, tightly wrapped and well-sealed package just as Jubal led his chosen mount into the front yard. The name and address of a man in Cheyenne was printed on the front of the package in bold black ink.

Jubal merely glanced at the address before sliding the package into one of his saddlebags. Then Agnew had retreated to the stoop just as his wife led Andy from the house.

'He wanted to say goodbye,' the woman said nervously to her husband.

Agnew smiled expansively and laid a gentle hand on the boy's shoulder. 'Only natural, my dear. Him and Mr. Cade have been through a lot together.'

'Good luck, Jubal,' Andy called, raising a slim arm in farewell.

Jubal smiled, aware the boy could not see the expression. So he emphasized the lightness of his tone. 'I figured that lady deserted me at poker, but she came through, Andy,' he replied. 'Got a feeling she'll stick with me for a while.'

He nodded to Ben Agnew and touched the brim of his derby towards the woman. She smiled warmly.

'Take care,' Agnew urged.

Jubal clucked to the stallion and tapped his heels against the animal's sides. He rode out of the yard and heard the front door of the house close. He jerked on the reins to head the horse west on the turnpike and glanced back at the big house. Two windows shafted warm light out into the clear, cold air of a winter's midnight. A small shadow fell across one of the windows and became still. The fact that Andy could not see through the lace curtains was immaterial. Jubal knew the boy would be straining his ears to catch the clop of hooves until they faded into the distance. He remembered what he had said to the boy about not wasting any time and abruptly thudded his heels hard against the horseflesh. The stallion snorted and lunged into a gallop.

Jubal held the animal at full speed until he was sure he was out of earshot, then slowed to a canter. Cheyenne was a long way off, across Missouri, Kansas and Colorado Territory's north-east corner. He aimed to make it a fast round-trip, but galloping his horse into the ground on the first night out wasn't the way to achieve this. So he held the big horse to a steady canter for the first two miles on the turnpike. Then, after swinging to the north along a spur trail he eased back to a walk.

The moon hung low in the sky, waxing towards half. The brightness of its blue-tinged light promised a frost before dawn and when the prairie did begin to reflect the moonglow from a million sparkling crystals of frozen moisture, Jubal experienced doubt about his decision to make such an early start. But it had seemed like a good idea at the time, simply because it allowed him to have no second thoughts about agreeing to take the job Agnew offered.

It seemed straightforward enough and Agnew's reason for choosing Jubal to undertake it sounded valid.

Agnew was expanding his ranching activities, preferring to buy established properties and herds rather than starting from scratch in untamed country. He had taken a look at some spreads in Wyoming and made an offer for several thousand acres outside of Cheyenne. The owner had taken a long time thinking over the offer and when he finally agreed to accept, Agnew was back in St. Louis. The acceptance arrived by mail with an urgent request that the purchase price be despatched immediately, in cash. Business commitments held Agnew in St. Louis and he was not prepared to trust such a large sum to either the express company, railroad or any of his help.

But Jubal Cade was the perfect messenger. He needed a lot of money in a short time and the reason he wanted it made him totally trustworthy.

'You gotta understand the way I have to look at it, son,' Agnew had said over dinner at the hotel. 'Unless you had the boy ... if you didn't have Andy to care for, I wouldn't trust you with a hundred grand any further than I could see you. But the way you feel about him, you wouldn't ride off into the blue yonder without making sure he gets the medical attention he needs: not for ten million dollars you wouldn't do that.'

Now, as Jubal rode through the night with the ground growing whiter by the minute and his expelled breath misting like smoke billows, he realized that his relief at being offered a way out of his difficulties had clouded his judgement. In retrospect, Agnew's trusting attitude seemed hollow: his wife's warm smile appeared as a mask for her true feelings; and Andy's silent sadness was a reflection of pity for Jubal rather than the surface reaction to his own depression.

In the cold, white night, Ben Agnew's tale smelled of deceipt. Honest business transactions involving such a high turnover as this one were not undertaken on a cash basis. Bankers' drafts were used. The more Jubal thought along these lines, the more he was convinced that Agnew had involved him in a crooked deal. Especially in view of the rate for the job.

But, as dawn broke, he decided to ignore the results of his long period of assessment. Andy had to go to the Lenz Clinic and the five thousand dollars would enable him to do so. That was the only moral issue which concerned Jubal and if his conscience bothered him when this was achieved, he would just have to learn to live with the guilt.

Not until the sun hauled itself clear of the horizon and started to evaporate the frost did Jubal become conscious of his weariness. He had been riding for six hours through an ice cold night following a day weighted heavily by anxieties. Despite the deep thoughts which had concerned him from almost the moment he left the Agnew house, he had not been riding aimlessly. Agnew had provided him with a map and Jubal had kept to a course he had plotted in his mind. The route lay north west to the bank of the Missouri River, then due west to Jefferson City. The turnpike would have made for easier travelling, but Jubal elected to stay off it for a good reason – road agents. They operated on the main routes into and out of St. Louis just as they did around any other large city. And although there was no way hold-up men could be aware of the contents of Jubal's saddlebag, he was not about to court trouble if it could be avoided.

So he stayed on the side trails connecting remote settlements and small farms. And it was into a tiny community, called River's Bend, that he rode at a point where tiredness threatened to overtake him while sitting in the saddle. The village was composed of three dirt farms clustered around a church, saloon and general store in a grove of oak and elm trees. The community drew its name from being sited at an elbow turn in the Missouri. The mournful tolling of the church bell announced the presence of the village before Jubal rode clear of the timber and saw the huddle of single storey wooden buildings.

Some twenty people – perhaps the entire population of River's Bend, he thought – were grouped at the side of the church. And he realized the reason for the bell's sad sound: it was tolling the death knell. The final note rang out as Jubal walked his horse into the square formed by the buildings. The stallion's well-shod hooves made a lot of noise on the frozen, hard-packed ground and several heads were turned towards Jubal. But then the priest began to intone the burial prayer in slow-spoken Latin and all eyes returned to the plain pine casket as it was lowered into the open grave.

Jubal took off his hat and swung down to the ground, surprised at how stiff he felt after the long but relatively easy ride. He led the stallion across the square to the saloon, which was directly opposite the graveyard at the side of the tiny church. There was a water trough adjacent to a hitching post. He had to break a half inch of ice with the heel of his boot before the stallion could drink. It made a loud crack, but not a single pair of eyes were raised to seek out the cause of the sound. The droning voice of the priest seemed to have a hypnotic effect on his parishioners. Jubal hitched the stallion to the post and unfastened the saddlebags. Then he unhooked his valise, slid the Spencer from its boot and went to the door of the nameless saloon. The door was closed against the weather but not locked to keep out customers.

Warmth hit Jubal like an invisible barrier. But a barrier that was easy to pass through into even greater warmth. It emanated in luxurious waves from a pot-bellied stove glowing red in the centre of the small, crudely-furnished saloon. There were just a half-dozen tables, each surrounded by four chairs,

36

spread in front of a short bar counter. Shelves behind the bar were sparsely stocked with bottles and glasses. Early morning sunlight shafted in through a single window beside the door. Dust motes, raised by Jubal's boots, floated in the light.

When he had lowered himself gratefully into a rickety chair at a table on the far side of the stove, Jubal was able to see out through the window to the group gathered in the grave-yard. There were six men and fourteen women, all dressed in sombre black. The men were hatless in the biting chill of morning and the women wore veils over their faces.

The heat from the stove threatened to close Jubal's eyes with drowsiness and the scene beyond the window had, in fact, become a blur when the death knell clanged again. He jerked up his head and forced his eyelids wide. The funeral service was over and the group of mourners were dispersing. Except for two men who moved away only so far as the side of the church. Here they collected two shovels and returned with them to the grave side. They began to shovel the earth into the hole. It fell in frozen clods and even from inside the saloon Jubal could hear the hollow thuds on the casket.

Then the door opened and a man and a woman entered, the woman throwing her veil back over her head. They both appeared to be in their late thirties, or were perhaps younger and showing signs of being used badly by life. The woman had hair and eyes as black as her dress. The man was red-faced and very thin with coldly glinting grey eyes. He wore a threadbare suit with a shirt buttoned to the throat and no tie.

'We ain't serving no drinks here today, mister,' he greeted flatly.

The woman closed the door, cutting off the icy draught that had scythed through the saloon.

'How about coffee?' Jubal asked, rising in deference to the woman, then dropping back on to the chair again.

'Folks around here make their own,' the man replied, mov-ing wearily across the saloon towards a gap at one end of the bar. His wife – she wore a wedding band so Jubal made the

37

assumption – trailed after him with her thin shoulders stooped.

Jubal looked over his shoulder at them, as the man went from sight through a doorway. The woman halted and glanced at him.

'I'll be making some. No trouble to pour another cup.'

They both had voices in keeping with their appearance: and that of the saloon – even the whole village. Weary and disillusioned.

'Kind of you, ma'am,' Jubal replied.

She did not respond as she turned and went in the wake of her husband. Jubal looked out of the window again as the bell ceased to toll. The casket was now fully covered by earth and the frozen top soil had all been shovelled in. The work of the men was easier and they did it more quietly. When they had finished, having formed the displaced earth into a neat mound, they returned their tools to the side of the church and looked towards the saloon, frowning. They exchanged a few words, reached a mutual decision and started across the square.

The dark-eyed, careworn woman delivered a cup of coffee to Jubal just as the door opened to admit the two men and an icy blast. They moved over the threshold fast and slammed the door, relishing the warmth.

'Morning,' Jubal greeted. Not brightly. His tone was merely polite. He nodded his thanks to the woman.

'It is,' the shorter and elder of the two men replied. 'But it's not a good one in River's Bend.'

He was bald with eyes which were too small for the round fleshiness of his face. His companion was about ten years younger, in his mid-thirties, gawkishly tall and thin with a lean, funereal face which fitted him for the work he had been doing.

'Guess you ain't serving nothing stronger than coffee today, Mary Anne?' the tall man asked.

The woman's mouth tightened into a grim line. 'You oughta know better than to ask, Tom Golding!' she hissed. 'You just this minute finished covering that poor girl in the ground.'

'Cold work, Mary Anne,' the other man said dully.

'Welcome to sit by the stove,' the woman replied curtly as she swung around and went through the gap in the bar and disappeared into the doorway.

The men advanced to the table where Jubal sat and dragged two chairs close to the glowing stove. They nodded to him, then concentrated upon warming the palms of their hands.

'Who died?' Jubal asked after taking several sips at the coffee, enjoying the warmth it spread through his belly.

'Was killed,' Golding growled in reply. 'Ginnie Fletcher. Nathan's daughter.'

'He's a stranger,' the elder man pointed out. 'Names don't mean nothing to him.'

'Don't know and don't care,' Golding rapped out. 'Why should he? Ain't none of his business.'

'Could be, if he figures to stay sat here for long,' the other responded.

Golding frowned, then shrugged. 'Lowell's got no quarrel with him. He'll be left alone.'

'Flying lead ain't got a mind of its own, Tom. Smacks into anything or anybody happens to be in the way.'

Jubal sipped some more coffee then lowered the mug to the table. He lit a cheroot to try to ward off weariness. 'Trouble coming?' he asked evenly.

Golding stared hard at Jubal, his expression unfriendly. Then he gave a grunt which seemed to go some way towards relieving his feelings. 'Kurt's the one seems set on running off at the mouth,' he said, returning his gaze to the glowing stove.

Kurt cleared his throat. 'Just reckon you ought to know what's goin' to happen in River's Bend, mister,' he said. 'Man shouldn't meet trouble with his eyes closed.'

Jubal struggled to keep his open. 'Something to do with the girl you just buried?'

A sad-faced nod as Mary Anne came in from the doorway at the rear, carrying two more mugs of coffee. She brought them to the table.

'Jed says I've to put nothing in them,' she announced. 'Every man will need a clear head when Lowell and his boys get here.'

She returned behind the bar and stood there, in a position to serve but her wooden expression deterring anyone from asking for a drink. Kurt and Golding tried their coffee and grimaced at the unlaced heat of the brew.

'Sam Lowell operates the biggest wheat spread in the State of Missouri,' Kurt said dully. 'About ten miles west of here. Got a son. named Douglas. Did have one, 'til last night, that is. Real mean bastard. Been setting his cap at Ginnie Fletcher long as he was old enough to feel his oats. But Ginnie was never that kind. Religious girl. Reckoned to enter one of them there nunnery places back east.'

'Convents, they're called,' Mary Anne put in flatly.

'Yeah,' Kurt agreed. 'Last night Doug Lowell came into town and got drunk in here. When he left we figured he was heading for home. But he went to the Fletcher farm instead. Nathan was in here. We heard some screaming and we went running. But we was too late. He'd got every last stitch of clothes off that girl. Had her backed up against the wall. But Ginnie grabbed a knife.' He shook his head, as if in disbelief. 'Nobody'd ever figure a girl like that would be so strong. Stuck it in him. Up to the hilt. In his belly.'

'Terror ain't something just in the mind,' Mary Anne said.

The shaking of Kurt's head became a nodding. 'Maybe. She stayed strong for a bit more. Nobody's sure iffen it was her shame at what the Lowell boy did to her or iffen it was because everybody in River's Bend saw her nakedness. But that little girl just pulled out that knife from the boy and sank it into her own heart.'

'She was only fifteen,' Golding said softly.

'And the boy's father isn't accepting that's the way it happened?' Jubal suggested.

'He wouldn't even iffen we'd given him the chance,' Kurt

40

replied as Mary Anne's husband emerged from the rear of the saloon. 'But we just packed his boy's body on his horse and spooked him. Horse knows the way home. Had to carry the boy out there dead drunk lots a times.'

Jed had two Winchester rifles which he rested on the bar.

'Whole town agreed to handle it that way,' Mary Anne said before Jubal could speak. 'Ben Lowell ain't a reasonable man. His hands have caused enough trouble and heartache in this town, mister. Ginnie Fletcher getting killed was the last straw.'

'So I reckon you ought to ride out before Lowell and his men ride in,' Kurt said earnestly to Jubal.

Jubal was thoroughly warm now, from the fire in the stove and the coffee. He was still hungry and still bone-deep tired. But not to the extent that he could not think clearly. Apart from the town's troubles being no concern of his, he had a job to do.

'Obliged for the information,' he said, making to gather up his gear.

Galloping hoofbeats sounded in the distance.

'Come too late,' Golding rasped, springing to his feet.

Because he was older, Kurt's movements were slower. But he made good time to the door in the wake of Golding as Jed and Mary Anne snatched up the Winchesters. The hoofbeats swelled in volume as shouts rang across the square outside. The two men had left the door open and chill air swept in to dissipate the heat from the stove. The saloon owner and his wife came out from behind the bar and ran forward, ignoring Jubal. Jed took up position in the open doorway while his wife stood at the side of the window. Both jerked the lever actions of their rifles.

For a few moments, the square seemed to be filled with men and women scurrying in every direction as they shouted to each other. Then it was empty and silent. Eerie in the bright sunlight of morning. The hoofbeats swelled, seeming to set up a visible vibration in the air. Jed peered out and drew back quickly.

'He's got them all,' he reported. 'Twenty, at least.'

'Expected,' Mary Anne responded flatly as the approaching riders slowed their mounts.

The horses were reined to a halt, snorting and stamping.

'Jed!' Mary Anne said urgently.

'Yeah?'

'Three more. Trail from the east.'

Jed looked in that direction and withdrew his head quickly. 'More strangers. They'll get the drift soon enough.'

'Who killed my boy?' a voice boomed.

Jubal got up from his chair and carried his gear to the gap in the bar. He went through and moved along until he had his back to the ill-stocked shelves. He dropped the saddlebags and valise on the floor and rested the Spencer across the counter top.

'Ginnie Fletcher!' a man called in reply.

'Send her out here!'

Although he was farther away from the window now, Jubal had a better view through it. He could see almost the whole western side of the square. Ben Lowell was a grey-haired man of sixty or more. He was tall and thin and sat rigidly upright in the saddle, positioned at a halfway point along a line of grim-faced men. Every rider held a Winchester resting across the neck of his horse.

'She's in the graveyard, Lowell,' the town's spokesman answered. 'Your boy got drunk and tried to rape her. She killed him, then turned the knife on herself.'

The sun shone full into the faces of the mounted men. Lowell's features were pallid under their weathered complexion. His thin lips compressed tightly as he listened to the explanation. His narrowed eyes flicked towards the fresh mound at the side of the church then away.

'Dig her up and show me!' he ordered.

Several gasps merged into a single sound. A woman shrieked in horror.

'She died in naked shame,' the spokesman retorted. 'We ain't about to dishonour her again now she's dead.'

Lowell pulled himself even more upright in the saddle and a patch of bright red showed at the centre of each cheek. 'And I am not about to believe what you say about my son. You had your chance.'

He fired the Winchester, swinging it up from the rest and towards the saloon. The bullet shattered a window pane. The sounds of the shot, of the breaking glass and of Mary Anne's scream merged into one which acted as a signal for an explosive fusillade. Every man in the line swung up his rifle and fired, sending a spray of bullets across the square, smashing through glass, burrowing into wood and ripping through flesh.

Mary Anne was hit in the face and staggered back from the window, covering her wound with her hands. But, as more screams rose and another burst of rifle fire exploded, the blood gushed through her fingers and she crashed across a table and lay still. One rider was lifted from his saddle, chest opened up in three places as the other men heeled their animals forward.

Jed sent two wild shots out through the door, then whirled and rushed to his wife's side. Jubal stayed where he was, knowing from the utter stillness of her body and the sudden halt to the fountain of blood from her forehead wound that the woman was dead. Jed tried to lift her, tears streaming down his face as he looked at Jubal. But Jubal had no time to confirm the man's already certain knowledge.

Outside, the line of riders had broken into groups to face each side of the square from the centre. Two of them slumped to the ground, hit by wild shots from the surviving citizens of River's Bend. Then the massed Winchesters cracked and Jubal flung himself to the floor.

Jed was hit by four bullets, taking them in the back and he was hurled hard across the body of his wife by the impact. The table could not support the extra weight and collapsed with the ugly tearing sound of splintering wood.

Then it was over. The silence came with the abruptness of the first shot that had opened the gun battle.

'Enough!' Ben Lowell bellowed, thrusting his rifle high into the air.

His men backed up their horses to form an outward facing circle around him. Their rifles swung back and forth, raking the facades of the buildings. Their watchful eyes glinted in grim faces.

'How many are dead?'

A voice began to call out names. As Jubal straightened up he recognized the tones of the priest. Twenty-two names were called. Fourteen replied. Like Mary Anne and Jed, Tom Golding and Kurt failed to respond. The name Nathan Fletcher drew silence for an answer.

Lowell gave an emphatic nod. 'Vengeance is mine,' he announced. Then he spoke softly to a man at his side. This man designated two more and the three dead riders were slung across the saddles of their horses. The reins were taken up.

Then, without another word, Lowell urged his horse from out of the centre of the circle and slammed in his heels. His men trailed after him, matching his gallop, out along the trail stretching to the west. As the sound of the massed hoofbeats faded into the distance more horses were ridden into the square. Not many, and at an easy walk. The priest shuffled out from the church, ashen-faced, head bowed and hands clasped together at his chest.

When Jubal reached the doorway of the saloon he saw that all fourteen survivors of the battle had shuffled out into the sunlight. The three horsemen Mary Anne had seen riding in from the east were halted in front of the town's single store. They looked indifferently at the scene before them: the shocked survivors, the four bodies sprawled across door steps and window sills and the still wet bloodstains where Lowell's men had died. Then they looked hard at Jubal with his odd assortment of burdens.

'Do we have any wounded?' the priest asked.

There was a general shaking of heads.

'Just dead folks, it seems, father,' a man replied at length.

44

Jubal's cool brown eyes returned the stare of the trio of riders and each of them gave a curt nod. Simple acknowledgement, neither friendly nor otherwise.

'Looks like we picked a bad time to ride through, padre,' the smallest of the three riders drawled.

'The time in River's Bend has never been good,' the priest replied without looking at the men. 'I advise you and your companions to keep riding. For as far as it is necessary to go before the name Ben Lowell means nothing.'

The small man whistled. 'So that was Ben Lowell. Obliged to you, padre.'

He urged his horse forward and the two others followed him, swinging around in a curve to by-pass the grieving group. Clear of the square, all three looked back over their shoulders and Jubal could not shake off the suspicion that they were surveying him rather than anybody else in sight.

'You, too, my son,' the priest called to Jubal. 'Lowell is an evil and bitter man. It is possible he may reflect on what has happened and decide that eight deaths are not enough to make up for the loss of his son.'

'You people are staying,' Jubal said.

'As we always have,' the priest replied. 'Because it is our home.'

Jubal eyed the chestnut stallion which had somehow escaped the hail of bullets and remained hitched to the post. 'Horse and me are both about done in, padre,' he said. 'Like to rest up here for a few hours.'

'A man is free to risk his life for whatever purpose he chooses,' the priest answered. 'There is a room at the rear of the saloon which Jed and Mary Anne used to rent to travellers. And a stable out back. If you must stay, the facilities are yours.'

'Appreciate it,' Jubal responded, moving out of the saloon to unhitch the stallion.

'You must be tired,' a man muttered wryly.

'Dead tired, maybe,' another put in. 'Iffen Lowell and his boys come back.'

But Jubal was not concerned with the embittered local farmer. As he led his horse around to the back of the saloon he glanced out along the west trail. On the crest of a hill beyond the grove of trees surrounding town the three horsemen were halted in a tight group. And although the distance was too great for their faces to show up clearly, Jubal had the certain feeling that he alone was the object of their interest.

CHAPTER FOUR

Ben Lowell did not return to River's Bend while Jubal slept off his exhaustion in the back room of the saloon. When he woke it was to the familiar sound of the tolling funeral bell and the knell continued to split the peace of the afternoon as he cooked himself a meal, using his own supplies but Mary Anne's kitchen.

Beyond the grimed window which overlooked the back of the saloon towards the slow moving river, the afternoon appeared as brightly cold as the morning. It proved to be so when he carried the saddlebags, valise and Spencer across to the double-stall stable at the side of the yard. The stallion had slept and fed as well as the rider and seemed anxious to gallop away from River's Bend the moment Jubal swung into the saddle. His ears were pricked to the mournful, monotonous clang of the bell and his nostrils flared, sucking in the scent of death and expelling clouds of grey mist.

Jubal held him to a nervous walk along the side of the saloon, shooting a glance towards the hill crest west of town. It was deserted as the sun dipped towards it. The square was equally deserted, the surviving citizens of River's Bend choosing to suffer their grief in private. There were now nine mounds of fresh earth beside the tiny church.

'Appreciate the hospitality!' he called against the sombre background noise of the bell.

A door creaked open and drew his attention to the arched entrance of the church. The priest stood in the porch, looking more stooped and much older than a few hours ago. 'We are good people, my son,' he intoned. 'Our willingness to give what help we can to others is not influenced by their unwillingness to help us. It was not your fight.'

The words made Jubal feel as cold inside as the icy air

47

chilling his hands and stubbled face. Even though the final comment negated the implication of criticism and there was compassion in the melancholy face of the old priest, Jubal sensed other, less charitable eyes focused upon him. But a glance around the square showed only closed doors and blank windows. With an angry gesture, he wheeled the stallion and urged him into a gallop out along the west trail.

The truth hurt only because a few weeks ago the priest's words would have been a lie. No, not a lie. It would not have been necessary for the stooped old man to speak them. Somehow – it was futile to consider the possibilities after the event – he would have tried to help the people of River's Bend. For both his basic nature and his calling as a medical practitioner had made him a man dedicated to helping others.

But he had changed. In a few short weeks his dream of trying to ease the hardships and suffering of the kind of people who lived in River's Bend had been shattered. He had been aware of this before: but not until the priest spoke his final words did he stare his new self full in the face.

His anger was expended as he reached the top of the rise and looked ahead across a vast plain of pastureland and fields ploughed ready for new planting. He had suspected what kind of man he had become and the events in River's Bend had proved it. Altruism had died with Mary and if any last threads of his former character had been left hanging, the knowledge of his responsibilities towards Andy Prescott had severed them completely. Faced with the twin task of caring for the boy and killing the man who murdered his wife, nothing else mattered. And since River's Bend offered him no assistance in achieving either of these aims, he owed the town nothing.

He tested this conclusion on himself and felt not the slightest twinge of guilt. Just as, at the start of the trip to Cheyenne, the suspicion that he was involved in an illegal deal had caused no pangs of conscience, so he accepted what he had become and, as he rode down the long hill and started along the arrow-straight trail across the plain, he drew back his lips to show the broken-toothed grin. A new sense of freedom, as fresh as the chill air drifting across the face of the bright after-noon, made him almost light-headed with relief.

But, abruptly, it was pushed aside by a strong sense of danger. Ahead, the trail continued in a perfectly straight line, running between neatly ploughed fields. The river swung away to the north, glinting only occasionally when Jubal rode over the top of a gentle rise. The lone rider seemed to be the only movement on the vast plain. But then, as Jubal sensed the threat, there was another. A flock of pigeons panicked into flight from a stand of timber into which the trail disappeared about a quarter of a mile ahead. It was late afternoon now and the sun shone directly into Jubal's eyes from its position low down in the western sky. It threw long, deep shadows from the trees. But Jubal knew there were men at the edge of the timber and as he cantered his horse closer he checked that the Spencer would not snag if drawn from the boot. The image of the three horsemen on the hilltop was imprinted on his mind.

But, as he rode into the shadows, slowing the stallion to a walk and losing the glare of the sun, he saw there were just two men on the trail. He did not recognize them. Both were young with arrogantly handsome faces. He placed them in their early twenties and decided they were more self-assured than youngsters of that age ought to be.

'Hope you're gonna stop, mister,' the one on the left said easily. He was clean-shaven except for the untidy beginnings of a black moustache along his upper lip.

He levelled a Winchester at Jubal. His partner did the same. He matched the other's height of about six feet but was more thickly set. He had eyes of the brightest blue. They looked as if they had been there some time. Unsaddled horses were tethered in the brush and the grey ashes of a former fire were piled at the side of the trail, under a sooted tripod. Both men wore long, thick topcoats with gunbelts hitched on the outside. Earmuffs jutted down from under the brims of their low-crowned hats.

'You've got a couple of good reasons why I should,' Jubal

49

replied evenly, reining in his horse.

The man with the piercing eyes laughed harshly. 'Stop you dead, mister. If you've a mind try riding on without paying the toll.'

'Toll?' Jubal asked without surprise.

The man starting the moustache nodded. 'You been on Lowell land for better than three miles. That you get for free. Go farther and it'll cost you ten dollars.'

Jubal sighed. 'And I figured to stay off the turnpike for fear of getting held up.'

Both men tightened their mouthlines and fixed Jubal with hard stares. 'This ain't no hold-up, mister,' Blue Eyes rasped. 'We're Lowell hands, hired to collect tolls for the boss.'

'He's not going to make a fortune on this trail,' Jubal answered.

Both men were on his right, standing about three feet apart, level with each other. He made as if to dismount with slow reluctance, but as his left leg arced over the back of the stallion, he powered into speed. He snapped his right leg straight and pushed against the stirrup. Then he kicked free. The Winchesters were not cocked and he doubted the men had orders to kill for the sake of a ten dollar toll. Surprise froze them into immobility for a moment. By which time Jubal was in mid-air, leaping down between the gun barrels before they could be swung towards him. He curled a hand around the cold metal of each barrel and hit the ground in a crouch, forcing the muzzles down. Each man gave a snort of alarm and tried to lever a shell into the breech of his rifle. But they were only halfway through the action when Jubal started a backward roll, curving his back and lashing up with his legs.

Gripping the rifles by the barrels and levers, the two men were jerked forward and down. Then Jubal's boot toes thudded into their bellies and hooked under their gunbelt buckles. Snorts of alarm became yells of pain, then cries of terror as they were lifted clear of the ground and sailed up and over the doubled form of Jubal. Breaking their fall was suddenly more important than retaining a grip on their rifles and they surrendered the guns to their assailant.

As the men thudded hard against the frozen ground beneath the stamping hooves of the chestnut stallion, Jubal powered himself to his feet. He dropped one of the Winchesters and swung the other around to the aim as he whirled towards the men. Both were in the process of rolling on to their backs, reaching down with numbed hands to draw.

The rifle's lever was hanging down from below the trigger. Jubal snapped it closed and fired. A yard separated the men. The bullet burrowed into the ground at a centre spot, kicking dirt at their faces.

'You want to believe I missed?' Jubal asked as both men became utterly still and he jacked a fresh shell into the breech. He had fired from the hip. Now he raised the rifle to nestle the stock against his shoulder and aimed along the barrel. He swung from side to side, raking the muzzle from one frightened face to the next and back again.

'Hell, mister,' New Moustache blurted out. 'Let's nobody get hurt for ten lousy bucks.'

'And you ain't even from River's Bend,' Blue Eyes augmented.

'Makes a difference?' Jubal asked, continuing to swing from side to side.

'Sure does,' Blue Eyes replied hurriedly. 'Mr. Lowell's got a big beef with the folks in that town.'

'I heard,' Jubal said.

'Yeah? Yeah, well. Them folks gotta use this trail to get to Sedalia. To sell what they raise on them scrub farms and buy supplies.'

All their arrogant self-assurance was gone now. The swinging Winchester held them tight against the ground as if they were physically pinned there.

'Kill a few and break the rest,' Jubal said evenly.

'Reason it should bother you?' New Moustache asked nervously, screwing his eyes around to treat his partner to an angry stare.

'Maybe the fact that you caught me in the net,' Jubal told them.

'You can go through without paying, mister,' Blue Eyes offered.

'Appreciate that,' Jubal replied.

'Lunkhead!' New Moustache muttered to his partner.

'Unbuckle the gunbelts and stand up,' Jubal instructed.

The men did as they were ordered. Because of the cold and the numbing effect of slamming into the ground, their fingers were clumsy. But eventually the belts were freed and remained on the ground as the men rose. Jubal lowered the Winchester, but kept it casually aimed in their direction.

'Now turn around and take a walk.'

'Now look —' Blue Eyes snarled. On their feet and standing better than six inches taller than Jubal, both seemed to have recaptured some of their lost confidence.

'Looking and waiting,' Jubal cut in. 'And I've wasted more time than I can spare already.'

'What'll you do if we don't?' New Moustache taunted.

Jubal pursed his lips, then sighed. His deep-set brown eyes were impassive and his voice was toneless. 'Put a bullet in each of you. Ankle shots. Then rub some dirt in the holes. The horses I'll run off. Tetanus ain't a fun thing to have. Especially on top of a busted ankle. After a while you wouldn't even be able to shout for help.'

Both of them looked at Jubal and decided he wasn't capable of carrying out such a threat. But they were not that sure. By tacit agreement, they turned and began to amble along the trail. They passed close to the chestnut stallion, but if either one considered making a try for the Spencer jutting from the boot, he quickly decided against such a move. Jubal watched them until they were three hundred feet away before he moved to the side of the trail and altered his grip on the Winchester, Holding it by the barrel, he swung it against the trunk of a massive oak tree. The trigger guard crumpled and the trigger snapped. The men looked back over their shoulders at the sound, but kept walking. The second rifle suffered the same fate as the first. Then he drew a Colt from each holster on the ground and sailed it among the trees. The men were now more than a quarter of a mile away and still ambling along the trail. But when they looked back and saw Jubal freeing their horses they whirled and started to run for the trees.

Jubal did not speed up his movements as he mounted the stallion. But once in the saddle he dug in his heels hard and the animal lunged forward. The other two horses trotted obediently behind, their reins gripped in Jubal's hand.

'Turn 'em loose, you crud!' a voice shrieked in high-pitched anger.

Jubal showed his broken teeth in a grin of pure enjoyment. Another shout reached him, but distance and the intervening trees muffled it so that the words were indistinct. Not until he emerged on the far side of the timber did he release the reins and urge the stallion into a gallop.

For better than a mile, the loose geldings continued to follow. But then the ploughed ground gave way to lush pastureland and the animals veered to the side and halted to feed off the verdant grass. Jubal brought the stallion's pace down to an easy canter towards the sun, lower now and without glare as it changed colour from yellow to red in preparation for setting. In the softer light of approaching evening, Jubal saw a large house off to the right at a place where the Missouri curved south again. In the immediate area of the house the fields were smaller, fenced by recently painted picket barriers. A herd of healthy looking cows grazed in one field. A half dozen stud horses were corralled in another. Three proud bulls seemed discontent in a third.

The house was a big, two-storey structure with a great many outbuildings on one side. It's setting and richness reminded Jubal of the Lenz Clinic standing on the bank of another river. The trail no longer ran straight. Instead, it swung northwards, to sweep in front of the house which he knew had to be the home of Ben Lowell. Two more men were on the trail at this point, but in less aggressive attitudes than those back at the timber. They were leaning casually against a gate which gave access to the large front yard of the house. They had Winchesters but the rifles were held at rest. Gunbelts were worn underneath opened top coats. As Jubal neared them, slowing the stallion to a walk, he recognized the men from the line that had punished the citizens of River's Bend. Beyond them, in the fading sun and wedges of yellow prodding out from lighted windows in the house, more men moved about in the yard.

'Evening,' Jubal greeted flatly.

One of the men made no response. The other elevated his rifle with one hand, pointing it across the trail. There was plenty of room to ride around, but Jubal reined the stallion to a stop.

'Want something?' Jubal asked, looking casually from one grim face to the other.

'Pass?' the man with the raised rifle said.

'Thanks,' Jubal said and made to move his horse forward.

'You know what I mean,' the talker said, his voice altering from flat to hard. 'You got stopped by a couple of guys back along the trail. You pay?'

'I gave them what they were asking for,' Jubal replied easily.

'Give you a pass in exchange. Bit of paper. Receipt. To show you paid. You got it?' He spoke like a man who didn't like to use words.

'Guess not,' Jubal answered. 'Must have lost it.'

'How we know you paid?'

Jubal shrugged and glanced across the gate at the house. There were about a dozen men in evidence plus the two who had braced him. The similarity between Lowell's home and the Lenz Clinic warned him against standing up for a principle for the sake of ten dollars.

'He's paid,' the other man said, speaking for the first time.

54

'Little runt like him wouldn't 'a got through Larry and Matt.'

The Winchester was lowered. 'Okay, on your way. But you oughta kept that pass they give you.'

Jubal clucked his horse forward. 'Would have done that,' he said evenly as he rode by the two men. 'But I wasn't tolled.'

CHAPTER FIVE

He made good time to the state line, but weariness caught up with him at Kansas and he slept the clock around in a cheap hotel on 12th Street after his first bath and shave since leaving St. Louis. Had he not been so exhausted he might have paid more attention to the eerie feeling that he was being watched as he rode into town. Instead, he chose to ignore the mental warning, attributing it to the fact that Kansas City was the first community of any size he had come to on the trip. It was a crowded, bustling, rip-roaring place at ten o'clock at night. Inevitably, a great number of people saw him. But none of them could possibly know what was contained in the bulging saddlebag. Therefore it was his knowledge of the money in the package which tended to arouse his suspicion at every idle glance cast in his direction.

He reasoned himself into dismissing such suspicion as foolish and while he remained as alert as his weariness allowed, he did not pay particular attention to the individuals with whom he happened to clash eyes. Thus it was that he did not recognize a man leaning against the front of an Oak Street saloon as one of the three who had been at River's Bend during the gun battle.

The farther west he had ridden, the colder the weather had become. And, as he struck away from the Missouri the next morning a north wind was swirling across the Kansas flatlands, emphasizing the dangers of exposure. It carried spots of rain and low, grimly black clouds raced across the sky in imminent threat of bursting. The light was bad, almost murky. In it, the terrain spread before him appeared wild and inhospitable. Which, for the most part, it was. Kansas City, such as it was, represented the last outpost of any size in the Midwest. Now there was just desolate prairie and wild mountains

56

featured with isolated cow towns and widely spread farming communities. The country Mary and Jubal had been aiming for when they stepped ashore in New York harbour. The kind of country inhabited by the kind of people who would welcome a skilled doctor and surgeon. But that was all in the past.

Now, the rolling, windswept plain of Kansas represented a barrier to Jubal. And there was not a single soul anywhere on it who could expect help from him if the giving of such assistance slowed his progress.

The storm broke in late afternoon and forced him to make early camp in the lee of a low bluff at the side of a swollen stream. He was able to construct a crude tent from his bed blankets and some brush and sat out the crashing thunder and crackling lightning for two hours. Driving rain pelted into the shelter but attacked him with less severity than if he had been completely exposed to it. A fire was impossible, so he ate a meal composed of jerked beef and cold beans.

Then the storm moved south, the wind drove the rain in its wake. But it gusted more forcefully than ever as Jubal remounted and continued his journey: as if angry that the slight, soaking wet figure had survived the lashing fury of the cloud burst. Evening descended suddenly, the low light of the day scurrying away before the darkness of night. He stayed on the bank of the stream, swollen and fast-running with the teeming rain. The ground underfoot was soft and he allowed the stallion to make his own pace, hooves sinking deep into the mud and making an ugly wet sound as they were lifted out.

The rain ended in the early hours of the new day but the wind continued to roar in, threatening to tear Jubal out of the saddle. Thick cloud raced across the sky but there were no breaks in the cover. So the moon was merely a blurred sphere of dirty grey casting just enough light to show up the stream against the shadow upon shadow of the prairie terrain. But it was sufficient for Jubal's purpose, enabling him to follow a path that led in a generally north-western direction.

He rode with his head bent into the wind, crouching low in the saddle to get whatever cover was possible from the neck and head of his horse. Only occasionally did he look up, to check his bearings: relating his position to that of the low-hanging moon.

It was on such an occasion that he saw the farmstead. Far behind him the eastern skyline was just beginning to take on a tinge of grey, but the first light of day was not strong enough to reach ahead of him. So it was the weak moon that showed up the farm buildings: a small shack and a barn at the southern side of a low bluff. He probably would not have seen it from such a distance – it was still better than a mile away – but for the fact that his eye naturally followed the course of the rushing stream which cut across in front of the buildings before plunging into a thick, spreading stand of timber. For at first glance the shack and barn were just two more dark shapes against the looming backdrop of bluff and trees. But then a pane of window glass flashed a faint signal and he spotted the man-made symmetrical shapes among the less well ordered lines of nature.

The prospect of shelter from the elements and a dry place to rest pulled Jubal erect in the saddle and formed a smile of anticipation on his cold-pinched features. The stallion sensed the new spirit in his rider and responded eagerly to the demand for greater speed, cantering strongly over ground which seemed to harden by the moment under the onslaught of the drying wind.

Jubal's course along the edge of the stream took him through a gap in a broken-down fence: leaning posts which had rotted and trailed rusted, twisted wire. The fields on the property were as overgrown as the land outside. Other signs of long neglect became evident as Jubal rode closer to the buildings, eyeing them across the stream. A wagon with only a single wheel canted drunkenly in the drying mud outside the barn, which had a large hole in the roof. One of the double doors lay on the ground with grass growing through its cracks while the other hung at a crazy angle on one hinge, creaking as it swayed in the wind. The shack, which was only large enough to have two rooms at the most, had deteriorated at the same rate as the rest of the farmstead, but its owner had made some effort to halt the ravages of time and the elements. Two holes in the one-way sloping roof had been patched with tin sheeting and more than half the window panes had been broken and were now replaced by squares of cardboard. Several attempts had been made to prop up the sagging stoop awning. but it looked in imminent danger of collapse with each new tug of the wind.

'Could be we'd both be safer out in the open,' Jubal said softly to the horse as he pulled at the reins.

The animal pricked his ears, then plunged courageously into the white water and flying spray of the stream. It was about ten feet wide running through the farmstead, but no deeper than four feet at its centre. The stallion remained sure-footed all the way across. The wind was less strong in the lee of the bluff, but a lot noisier. It whined around the buildings with a mournful note and the creaking of barn door and shack stoop had an eerie quality. From the timber came the awesome sound of tortured branches scraping together.

Jubal stayed in the saddle and rode the horse into the barn. The sounds outside retreated as man and horse entered the insecure shelter which smelled of wood rot and damp mould. There was no feed, of course. But a plentiful supply of fresh water: the recent rain ran off the bluff and formed a meandering brook entering the barn under one wall and vanishing under another to enter the stream. Draughts of chill air swooped in from many directions, but the poor shelter at least precluded the worst of the biting wind.

Confident that there would be no owner to object, Jubal dismounted and unsaddled the stallion. Then he hitched the animal to a loft support as far away from the open doorway and hole in the roof as possible. He knew it would not hold the horse if he was determined to escape, but the stallion seemed to have no inclination to return outside into the teeth of the wind.

The eastern sky was a solid grey colour when Jubal stepped outside the barn and the dismal pre-dawn light seemed to emphasize the decrepitness of the farmstead. But the whining wind quickened Jubal's pace towards the shack. When he kicked open the door the shot cracked a full stop to the tortured creak.

Jubal flung himself sideways, releasing the heavy burden of the saddle with its appendages of bedroll, bulging bag and the valise. But despite the shock of the sudden attack he had the presence of mind to drag the Spencer from the boot as he slammed into the rotting timber of the stoop. He hit the boarding on his side, but did not remain still for a split second. Instead, he rolled on to his back, then arced his body and flipped up his legs. He worked the action of the Spencer as he completed the feet-over-head roll. As his boots slammed to the boarding, he used his elbows to power himself up into a crouch, rifle poised to swing towards a target. He was looking along the stoop, across the open front door of the shack with the hastily discarded saddle piled on the threshold. He could plainly see the neat hole in the cantle made by the bullet. There were two windows at the front of the shack and his roll had taken him under one of them. Five of the eight panes had been smashed and replaced by cardboard.

Now he held still, breathing shallowly and silently, straining his ears to pick up a sound within the shack. The heat of anger burned inside him and was manifested on his face: his eyes blazed and he could feel the skin stretched taut over his features, flaring his nostrils and compressing his lips. The rage was as much directed at himself for approaching the shack so openly as at the gunman for taking advantage of his carelessness.

'I know I didn't plug you, mister,' the man inside growled. 'You didn't fall right.'

Jubal had not seen him. Just the muzzle flash which had pinpointed him directly in line with the door. The voice gave nothing away in such a small place.

'You're out there on the left. Move and them boards'll set

60

up creaking that'll tell me just where you are.'

The greyness had spread to the entire sky now and was dropping a depressing light over the farmstead. The sound made by the wind was more mournful than ever and it seemed to invest the voice of the man with a funereal tone. Words of doom.

'Now, you move the right way and I won't shoot. It's the money I want and I figure that's in the nice fat saddlebag I can see.'

Jubal did not waste time thinking about the implication of what the man said: that he had a better reason for killing than a nervous trigger finger. Instead, he took a quick look around him, keeping his weight evenly balanced and not moving his feet. To go forward meant first passing the window and then the doorway. Behind him the end of the stoop was too far away. He would have to turn and then take at least two paces to reach it. As the gunman had warned, the creaking boards would give away his position. And if he had a rifle – which Jubal was almost certain he did have – the high velocity bullet would easily penetrate the damp-rotted wall of the shack.

So he went sideways. He powered himself out of the crouch and canted his body, springing low off the stoop. A second shot cut across the moan of the wind and showered him with black fragments of rotted wood as the shifting of his weight produced an anguished creak. But the bullet spun over his head and kicked up new spray as it hit the water of the stream. Jubal took the full impact of the dive on his left shoulder and grunted in pain. Another shot exploded, the bullet bursting clear of the wall and burrowing into the dirt of the yard. Had Jubal remained where he was for the pain to pass, he would have taken the bullet in his stomach. But he rolled against the urging of his own momentum, flinging himself towards the front of the stoop. In its foot-high cover, he snaked forward, propelling himself with his elbows and knees. He had to grit his teeth to keep a cry of pain trapped inside him every time strain was thrown on his bruised shoulder.

'I might have got you that time, you sneaky bastard!' his attacker yelled. The tone was different now. Still confident, but less booming. It had lost its casual ease as the speaker had to make an effort to bolster his self-assurance.

Jubal kept moving, snaking under the window, then crossing the more dangerous ground in front of the door. But the pile formed by his discarded gear provided additional cover and he dragged himself into the relative safety beyond without drawing more shots.

'But I don't reckon I did,' the man called.

It was no longer essential to stay flat against the ground now, but Jubal did so, reasoning he made less noise than he would on his feet. He reached the end of the stoop and snaked around it, swinging his legs and body so that he was stretched out full-length, looking along the front of the shack. A piece of furniture – or perhaps a box – scraped against the floorboards inside. Jubal rested his cold, taut cheek against the stock of the Spencer and sighted along the barrel, covering the entire front of the shack. He guessed the man inside had risen to his feet, knocking against whatever he had been crouched behind as he did so. He strained his ears, waiting for further sounds of movement. But what he heard was something totally unexpected – galloping hoofbeats. His eyes swivelled, to flick a gaze across the rifle stock: out over the yard and stream towards the boundary fence. Two riders were racing across the neglected fields, their bodies curving into the wind, heads held low.

'About frigging time!' the man in the shack bellowed.

His running footfalls rang against the floorboards and then he burst clear of the shack with a powerful leap. He sailed over the pile of gear and fired two shots while in mid-air. Both bullets dug up earth in the area where Jubal would have been had he held his position after springing from the stoop. The man hit the ground and gave a bellow that was part rage, part fear. He chose to pitch forward into a dive rather than run, his head whipping around as he went down.

Jubal saw his face and instantly recognized the man – the

62

smallest of the three who had shown such undisguised interest in him at River's Bend. Then he shot him, before the man had a chance to swing his Winchester and work the action. He took careful aim at the abruptly terrified face atop the falling body and squeezed the trigger. The bullet smashed through the man's upper teeth, exposed as his mouth was dragged open to explode a scream. Shards of enamel rained inside the mouth, then provided speckles of gleaming white in the cascade of blood that gushed out from the gaping hole in its roof. The man hit the ground as a corpse and the flood of white-spotted scarlet became a trickle.

The two riders angled across the stream, the pumping hooves of the horses sending up great spumes of spray. Wind caught the flying droplets and hurled them across the yard. Then bullets cracked out of the spray and showered Jubal with more wood splinters from the front wall of the shack. He swung the Spencer and sent a shot towards the riders as they splashed clear of the stream, a couple of hundred feet short of where he had crossed. Both went into a tight wheel, firing their Winchesters for effect as they galloped off at right angles to the stream, placing the shack between themselves and Jubal.

Jubal heard the sound of skidding hooves and the angry snorting of the horses as they were jerked to an abrupt halt. Then running footfalls against the wind-dried ground. He levered another shell into the breech and looked along the front of the shack towards the pile of gear in the doorway. The saddle had fallen in such a way that the bulging saddlebag was on top. It was tantalizingly close: dangerously far away. Jubal thrust himself upright, whirled and started to run – away from the shack. As he reached the tilted wagon, two rifle shots cracked and bullets ricochetted off the iron rim of the remaining wheel. He ducked down and sent a shot smashing into the far corner of the shack. One of the men had been in process of coming around the angle of the wall. He flung himself back into cover. Jubal whirled and leapt forward again. Bullets exploded through the wall of the barn as he disappeared behind it. There was a hundred feet wide strip of open ground to the trees. The barn covered him for three-quarters of the way, but then the two men rounded the corner. The first shot cracked past his head. Meant to kill, it acted as a warning. He pitched himself into a forward roll as the second shot sped towards him. Fate decreed the bullet should smack into the stock of the Spencer just as Jubal relaxed his hold to take a firmer grip. The heavy rifle was torn from his grasp. There was no time to retrieve it.

His feet touched ground again as another bullet cracked close to him, and smacked into the trunk of a tree ahead of him. It made a solid sound verifying Jubal's conclusion – if such evidence were necessary – that the cover of growing timber was to be preferred to the neglected rottenness of the farmstead buildings. He spurted forward in a crouching run, zig-zagging to left and right and two further shots cracked dangerously close to him. Yellow scars showed on the black bark of two trees. Then he was free of the open ground and crashing through the thick brush matting the area between the sturdy trunks. The noise he made was at one with the grating of branches as they ground together and the moaning of the wind scything through the timber.

Panting for breath and silently cursing the loss of the rifle, he pressed deeper into the wood, stumbling over snagging brush and bouncing off rearing tree trunks. Not until he was more than fifty feet from the edge of the trees did he halt and turn to look back the way he had come. The view in that direction was the same as all the others. Close growing trunks of oak, elm, ash and beech trees with the brush rising from knee to shoulder height between them. The farmstead and his pursuers were completely screened by the leafless tangle.

He leaned against a trunk and took deep breaths as he unbuttoned his topcoat low enough so that he could reach into his vest pocket for the Remington under-and-over. It was fully loaded with two .41 calibre shells, but Jubal knew better than to think of the simple two for two equation. The tiny gun was strictly a short-range weapon and he doubted luck would provide him with both men so easily.

But there was the possibility that they would not come into the timber after him – if they found the money in the saddlebag. Which had been his intention in abandoning his gear: to allow them to keep it for as long as it took him to catch up with them: with himself as the attacker backed by surprise. It was vitally important for him to get the package to Cheyenne: futile to die for it anywhere.

A rifle shot cracked. Severed twigs snapped and the bullet thudded into the solid obstacle of a tree trunk. Instinctively, Jubal ducked, gun hand thrusting out, finger curled around the double trigger. But the sounds were far over to the right. Wind robbed shouted words of clarity but he detected the chiding tone. A man being taken to task – or taking himself to task – for shooting at something that wasn't there.

Jubal used the jumble of sound as a signal to move, striking off to the left, away from where the shot had been fired. If the men had both plunged into the timber on a false trail, recovering the money was going to be easier than Jubal could have hoped. He kept moving in a straight line for a hundred feet, then swung to the right, heading back on a line that he judged would bring him out at the side of the bluff behind the farmstead. The going was hard through the snagging brush and he constantly looked in every direction, sweeping his gaze from tree to tree, alert for movement not caused by the wind.

Dawn was fully broken now and with no foliage to screen it, daylight dropped down through the skeletal branches with dangerous ease. But, Jubal reasoned as he pushed through the brush, the disadvantage of light acted against his pursuers as much as it did himself. Then he reached the edge of the timber and halted abruptly, pressing his body against a trunk. His brown eyes, the fires of rage long extinguished, raked the farmstead. His sense of direction had been right and he had reached open ground behind the shack. Thus, he could not see the sprawled body of the dead man, nor the valuable saddlebag. Just the blank rear of the shack and the barn. A movement caught his eye and he tensed. But it was only the horse of one of the men. The animal was moving around from the side of the shack, head down, tearing at an area of grass. The second horse trailed it.

Jubal stepped out from behind the tree, intent upon searching the ground for his rifle. He saw the mud-encrusted toecap of another man's boot and snapped up his head. The single black eye of a Winchester's muzzle met his surprised stare. He tore his gaze away and looked higher: into the face of a man wearing an evil grin of triumph.

'Old Russ's trick sure enough flushed you out, punk,' the man said evenly. 'Hate to kill an unarmed man.' He shrugged. 'But that's the way it goes sometimes.'

As the grinning man spoke, Jubal started to raise his arms in a gesture of surrender. But he made sure the back of his right hand was towards his captor. Then, as his hand came level with his shoulder, he twisted his wrist and flipped the tiny gun forward. His finger hooked around the trigger and the Remington cracked. The bullet thudded into the man's shoulder and his grin abruptly had a frozen quality.

'Other way, other times,' Jubal replied softly as the man flicked his gaze down to the spreading patch of blood on his coat.

Then the man emitted a bellow of anger as he met Jubal's level stare again. Jubal was a split-second ahead of the man in squeezing the trigger. The Remington's second bullet ploughed through the flesh at the side of the man's neck, sending out a wide spray of blood. The man was turning as he fired the Winchester and his aim was wide. The bullet smacked into wood and the man fell to his knees, dropping the rifle and using both hands to clutch at the blood-gushing wound on his neck. As he started to topple to the side, Jubal sprang forward, crouching to snatch up the Winchester.

Another rifle exploded: farther away, but the bullet was a lot closer, snicking a half circle of brim from Jubal's derby.

'Don't kill him, Russ!' the injured man shrieked in panic. 'I'm hurt. He's a doc.'

The shot had immobilized Jubal, freezing him in the crouch, his outstretched hand more than twelve inches away from the fallen rifle. Only his eyes moved, swivelling up to look along the tree line to where the second man had come into view. This man was fully erect, Winchester raised to his shoulder, drawing a bead on his target. The direction and rock-steadiness of his aim warned that he would not miss a second time. The range was under twenty yards. Close enough for Jubal to see the confusion and indecision in the eye behind the backsight.

'Don't move,' the man ordered.

'Figure it's your's to make,' Jubal answered.

'Russ, I'm bleedin' to death!' the man on the ground entreated.

'How bad's he hurt, Cade?'

Jubal swivelled his gaze towards the injured man and saw the agonized fear in the twisted expression. He kept his tone even and just loud enough to be heard above the moan of the wind: but he injected venomous spite into his stare. 'Reckon he's going to die.'

The man's anguish was vented in a pathetic groan and he began to tremble.

'Clarke dies, he'll have company,' Russ snarled, starting forward with the Winchester still aimed.

Jubal straightened up, letting the empty Remington fall to the ground. He dropped his arms to his side.

'You gotta help me, doc,' Clarke pleaded. 'There must be a chance.'

Russ halted six feet away and lowered the rifle. But he still held it two-handed, pointing at Jubal. He flicked a glance towards the injured man, and his grimace at the sight of the massive flow of blood from the neck wound seemed to hold something more than mere horror. Not sympathy or pity: greater than that. Compassion. His next words explained why.

'You're gonna do what you can to help my brother, mister.' His voice lost none of its threat for being low-keyed. 'Either to keep him from dying or make his dying easier.'

Clarke caught his breath, struggled with emotions and then lost. He began to sob.

'Dying's never easy,' Jubal replied.

'But it can be awful hard, mister. If I blast off both your feet and leave you here, you'll find out how hard.' As he spoke, he lowered the aim of the Winchester.

Jubal had no doubt the man would carry out his threat. 'Okay,' he agreed.

Clarke stopped sobbing. 'You'll take care of me, doc?'

'Your brother's argument is too strong for me, feller,' Jubal replied. 'If I went up against that I wouldn't have a leg to stand on.'

CHAPTER SIX

The compact strength contained within Jubal's slight frame
was evident from the ease with which he supported the sagging weight of the injured man. But neither Clarke nor Russ
was concerned with his physical prowess: it was his skill as
a medical practitioner that interested them. And even this was
of secondary importance as the three of them made slow progress towards the crude shack. For Clarke was filled with the
fear of death. While Russ concentrated upon watching his
captive to ensure he pulled no tricks.

Jubal learned something as he held Clarke with one arm
around his waist, his other hand clutching the injured man's
wrist at his neck. Whether from genuine fear that he was on
the brink of death or because he was the kind of man who took
his suffering seriously, Clarke played his helplessness to the
full. He allowed his head to drop forward, dragged his feet
and leaned almost all his weight upon Jubal. And since the
injured man's brother brought up the rear, Jubal was able to
grin with immunity at this trait: which augured well for his
survival.

At the shack, Russ moved ahead of Clarke and Jubal, calling for them to halt while he made a wide half-circle. He removed the barrier of the dropped gear by dragging it inside,
then gestured for the others to follow him in.

As Jubal had guessed, the shack boasted just two rooms.
One for living and cooking and the other for sleeping. The
only furnishing consisted of two crates at the rear of the living
room. The atmosphere was the same as in the barn – the
cold air rank with the taints of damp and rot.

'Lay out that blanket,' Jubal instructed, nodding towards his
bedroll. 'Over there by the grate. Then light a fire. You got
any cooking pots?'

Russ's mouth was compressed into a tight line.

'Yeah, we got pots,' Clarke groaned.

'I ain't running around doin' what you tell me!' Russ snarled.

Now that they were standing still, Clarke was resting all his weight against Jubal. When Jubal released him and stepped to the side, the injured man was taken completely by surprise. He crumpled to the floor like something suddenly melted. His cry of alarm was punctuated by a scream of pain as his holed shoulder thudded against the floorboards. Russ backed away, jerking the Winchester up to his shoulder.

'So let him die the hard way,' Jubal said softly, staring fixedly at the brother with the rifle.

'For God's sake, Russ?' Clarke implored, his grizzled face contorted by pain. 'Please?'

Russ remained frozen in the pre-killing posture for long seconds. 'What's he gonna be doin' while I'm doin' his biddin'?' he demanded at length.

Clarke was on his side, curled up into a ball. He straightened out his body, rolled over on to his back and unbuttoned his top coat. Then he reached clumsily around his body with his left hand and drew a Remington revolver from his holster. He sat up, grimacing. Then he pulled back the hammer and pointed the gun at Jubal.

'He ain't gonna be doin' nothin',' he pronounced coldly. 'Cepting gettin' himself killed if he tries any tricks.'

'That won't help you,' Russ pointed out.

Clarke shook his head. 'He won't try no tricks. Not with this iron on him. Nobody wants to die. I oughta know that.'

Russ considered the new situation for a few moments, then nodded his agreement. He went to work, unstrapping the bedroll from the saddle, doubling the blanket and spreading it out in front of the fire grate on the wall dividing the two rooms of the shack. He worked clumsily for he continued to hold the Winchester. Constant hateful glances in Jubal's direction told of his willingness to use the rifle at the slightest provocation.

Jubal stood in a relaxed posture, not moving. He divided his disinterested attention between the two brothers and the view of the yard through the open door. Out there he could see the awesomely unmoving body of the third member of the trio, sprawled in the pool of his own blood. The icy wind had frozen the thick, crimson liquid and the brightening morning light gave it a sheen of ice. The stream beyond flowed with less urgency now as it sucked the ground dry of rainwater.

Russ used the stock of the Winchester to smash the two crates, then laid and lit a fire.

'You watch him good, Clarke,' he warned before going outside to fetch the horses.

'Clarke and Russ who?' Jubal asked, backing off towards the fire.

The injured man eyed him with a mixture of suspicion and envy.

'Longstreet,' he growled.

'And him?' Jubal nodded towards the doorway.

Clarke was confused for a few moments and almost turned to see what Jubal was indicating. Then the realization of the dead man hit him. 'Ron Fairchild. Buddy of ours.'

Jubal had been standing with his back to the fire. Now he turned half towards it, flicking his gaze over the leaping flames. But Russ had attacked the crates with a vengeance, the crashing stock of the rifle smashing the wood into fragments. There was not one piece large enough to carry across the small room with any force. Then the clop of hooves drew his attention to the doorway again. Russ was leading the horses towards the shack. He hitched both sets of reins to the strongest support and then unstrapped the bedrolls and brought them inside.

'No problems?' he asked Clarke.

'We just introduced ourselves,' the injured man replied.

Russ gave a jerk of his head, ordering Jubal away from the fire. 'What's he care who we are?' he asked as Jubal moved and he went forward. He began to lay the two blankets on

71

top of the other one, taking the cooking and eating utensils out of the rolls.

'In case I have to fix any grave markers for you,' Jubal replied softly.

'You stop talking that way!' Clarke yelled. He leaned forward suddenly, thrusting his gun hand towards Jubal. The movement shot pain through his stiffening shoulder and he groaned.

'Excitement's not good for you,' Jubal told him evenly.

'Who's excited?' Clarke snarled. 'I'm full of lead! Why the hell should I be excited?'

Jubal glanced at Russ and found the man staring at him through slitted eyes.

'Shut up, Clarke,' he urged. 'You're excited. Cade's making you that way. You do anything else except tell him who we are?'

Clarke blinked. 'Told him Fairchild was our buddy is all.'

'Keep it that way,' Russ growled as he gathered up the two cooking pots and headed for the door.

'You trailed me a long way,' Jubal said when Russ was out of earshot.

Clarke could form his mouth into a line equally as tight and thin as his brother's expression of silent determination. He was like Russ in a lot of ways. Both were a little over six feet tall and thickly set. Both had pleasant, vaguely unintelligent faces in repose, with grey eyes and sallow complexions. But when they were angry both Clarke and Russ betrayed an ugly meanness that indicated a natural cunning. Clarke was about twenty-five and had thick growing black hair. His brother was at least five years his senior and looked as if he might be almost bald under his hat.

'Took you all that time to raise the courage?' Jubal posed.

Clarke did not like remaining silent. He grew red in the face, as if keeping his mouth tight closed interrupted his breathing. 'Shut up!' he blurted out.

Jubal shrugged. The fire crackled and the strength of the wind faded so that it ceased to moan around the buildings.

The barn door and stoop awning stopped creaking. Russ's footfalls were heavy on the frozen ground. He entered the shack slopping water over the brims of both pots. The Winchester was jammed under his armpit. He looked at the relaxed Jubal and his straining brother with ill-humour, but said nothing until he had set the pots on the fire.

'All yours now, Cade,' he growled, transferring the Winchester to a two-handed grip as he backed across to the door and kicked it shut. 'Patch him up good.'

Jubal stepped towards Clarke.

'Toss that iron over here!' Russ demanded.

Clarke seemed reluctant to part with the gun, then sighed and scaled it across the floor. It finished up at Russ's feet. He left it there. Jubal crouched down beside the injured man and began to remove his clothes. Each item caused Clarke pain as it was removed. With the topcoat and jacket it was simply the movement of his muscles that set his shoulder on fire. But in taking off the shirt and undervest the congealed blood tore at the wound to pile on new agony. Fresh blood oozed. Clarke filled the room with his groans and shrieks. But Russ did not tense into making the threat of the pointing Winchester stronger. He smoked a ready-made cigarette by hanging it at the corner of his mouth. Through the rising smoke, he looked at Jubal with something like incredulity in his grey eyes. Clarke had come very close to killing the man – and would not hesitate to try again if the circumstances were different. Yet the man was handling Clarke like a fragile baby: his actions gentle and a look of compassion on his face.

'Russ, he's murderin' me!' Clarke roared as the undervest came clear to reveal the ugly wound in the shoulder.

'Like I told you, shut up!' Russ barked. 'Cade's doin' what he has to.'

'It ain't you got a bullet!' Clarke retorted, allowing Jubal to help him across to the spread blankets before the now roaring fire.

'It was him should have had the bullet,' Russ answered

73

sourly.

Clarke stretched out on the blankets with a sigh, the relief at experiencing the warmth of the flames temporarily transcending the discomfort of pain.

'Need to get my bag,' Jubal said.

'Get it,' Russ instructed.

Jubal crossed to his saddle and unhooked the valise. The bulge in the saddlebag looked bigger than ever.

'*You* was supposed to plug *him*,' Russ reminded.

'Accidents happen,' Clarke excused, watching with fearful eyes as Jubal snapped open the valise and delved inside. 'I wasn't properly ready when you fired that shot.'

'Wasn't ready to fire it,' Russ replied absently, watching Jubal unfurl a piece of cloth and then lay out his instruments. 'I heard something move and I blasted at it. Turned out to be Fairchild's horse hitched to a tree.'

Using a pair of tongs, Jubal dropped three instruments into one of the bubbling pots.

'Kill it?' Clarke asked, licking dry lips.

'What's it matter?' Russ asked. 'Fairchild won't be needing it no more.'

Jubal moved to his saddle and removed his own cooking pot. He wrapped Clarke's blood-stained shirt around his hand for a mitten and poured boiling water into the pot.

'But I killed the horse,' Russ added. 'When I aim to kill, I kill.'

Clarke gulped. 'Hell, Russ!' he exclaimed. 'Don't make this guy nervous.'

Jubal winced as he plunged his hands into the water. He began to wash.

'Cade don't look like the kind of man gets nervous easy,' Russ answered.

Jubal ignored him and looked earnestly at Clarke. 'You ready to do some more yelling?' he asked.

'What the hell is that supposed to mean?' the injured man whined.

'That it's going to hurt, lunkhead!' Russ growled.

'Ain't you got nothin' you can give me?' Clarke implored.

'Your brother could smack you over the head with that rifle,' Jubal allowed. 'But that could lead to concussion and you've got enough problems for now.'

'Quit yakking and start digging, Cade,' Russ ordered.

Jubal nodded and emptied his washing water across the floor. He refilled the pot with fresh boiling water and took a pack of swabs from the valise. And once more he became simply a doctor working on a patient. Personalities did not matter as he undertook the treatment of the wound. He could not avoid hurting the man as he rinsed the bullet hole clean of old and new blood. Russ knew this and, amid his low-pitched groaning, Clarke appreciated the fact. When the wound was clean – a white area around a dark hole surrounded by the dirt-grimed flesh of Clarke's shoulder – Jubal began to wash the congealed blood from the neck wound.

The bullet had done little damage, furrowing a groove less than two inches long. It had erupted a great deal of blood and would leave a livid scar. But it had not stayed lodged in the flesh to threaten putrescence. Jubal dabbed some cleansing alcohol on to the wound, then applied salve.

The shoulder injury was a different proposition entirely. The lead had penetrated deep and stayed buried in the flesh. It could have done a great deal of damage and would continue to poison the man for as long as it remained in his body.

'That was the easy part,' Jubal said as he used the tongs to fish a probe from the bubbling pot on the fire. 'You want something to bite on?'

Clarke swallowed hard.

'Let him use his tongue,' Russ suggested wryly. 'Bites through it he won't be able to keep yakking the way he does.'

But it was only tough talk. Brotherly affection, or perhaps just the pleading look in Clarke's pained eyes, caused Russ to spit out the cigarette and cross to the fire. He unbuttoned his top coat then knelt down at Clarke's head. He rested the Winchester on the floor at one side of him. The butt of the

Remington jutted from his exposed holster on the other side.

'I'll hold him still, Cade,' he said.

Clarke was starting in horror at the metal probe, glinting in the firelight. Russ forced his brother's head down to look the other way, then applied pressure to the side of his head and his good shoulder.

'Hurts worse when you see,' Russ said, and nodded to Jubal.

Jubal inserted the probe into the torn flesh and Clarke screamed. His body began to convulse with the agony of the tormenting metal but Jubal thudded his knee across the arching stomach. Russ held the head and shoulder hard against the floor. The end of the probe scraped against the bullet. When he pulled the probe clear, fresh blood spouted.

'Bad?' Russ asked.

Jubal swabbed at the blood.

'I ain't gonna die, am I, doc?' Clarke pleaded.

'Everybody dies,' Jubal replied evenly, using the tongs to secure another probe from the boiling water.

'I mean now!' Clarke shrieked. 'Of this!'

'Not right now,' Jubal told him and nodded to Russ.

The elder Longstreet jerked the head over to the blanket again and Jubal sank both probes into the wound. Clarke screamed and the veins stood out, blue and pulsing, against his neck and forehead. His complexion became the colour of dirty snow and then he went limp.

'You killed him!' Russ bellowed, springing to his feet and drawing the Remington. It was cocked before it cleared the holster.

'He's passed out,' Jubal corrected softly, concentrating upon his task of loosening the bullet from the tissue in which it was embedded.

Russ was within a fraction of a second of squeezing the trigger. For a little longer his rage was manifested in tunnel vision and he could see nothing else except Jubal's hands clutching the glinting probes. But the soft-spoken words cut across the turmoil of his emotion and his slitted eyes raked to the spread form of his brother. He saw the shallow rise and fall of the hair-matted chest. Russ felt suddenly exhausted as the tension drained out of him.

Jubal did not notice the man. He was totally engrossed in his delicate task, gently tugging at the sunken bullet with the probes. Then, as soon as he felt free movement, he dropped the instruments and used the tongs to hoist a pair of long-stemmed forceps from the sterilization pot. Clarke continued to remain absolutely still apart from the regular rise and fall of his chest as Jubal secured a grip on the loosened bullet and drew it clear of the flesh. Droplets of blood fell away from the misshapen piece of metal and Jubal became aware of Russ turning away in revulsion as he examined the bullet. Quickly, he tossed the recovered shell into the heart of the blazing fire and completed treatment of the wound: swabbing up the new blood, cleaning the torn flesh and applying ointment.

Russ was watching him again, his expression anxious as his eyes followed the dexterous movements of Jubal's hands fixing the dressing in place over both wounds. 'He goin' to be okay, Cade?' he asked, stooping suddenly to snatch up the Winchester as Jubal straightened, massaging the small of his back.

Jubal looked down at the half-naked man sprawled on the blankets. The bullet had not gone too deep. It had torn the skin and displaced some tissue. Severed some fibres of the Pectoralis major and ruptured many blood vessels. It had stopped short of touching the scapula.

'With care and surgery,' Jubal replied, squatting down on his haunches and taking the second pot off the fire.

'You just give him that,' Russ growled.

'Did what I could under the circumstances,' Jubal replied. He started to wash the blood from his hands and his instruments. 'He's just got a deep scratch on his neck. So long as it doesn't become infected, it won't give him any trouble. Shoulder's not so simple. Bullet hit the bone. It shattered and part of the bone splintered.'

77

Because there was nothing else to use, he wiped the instru-ments on the cleanest section of Clarke's shirt.

'What's that mean?' Russ demanded.

Jubal sighed. 'I could only get the biggest chunk of the bullet out. Needs a hole bigger than the one he's got to get at the rest of the lead and the bone fragments.'

Russ considered the opinion for long seconds, and Jubal stood up again, after snapping closed the valise. The barrel of the Winchester elevated so that it continued to draw a bead on his heart.

'So make a bigger hole, Cade,' Russ said coldly.

Jubal shook his head. 'He wouldn't stay unconscious for long enough. Belting him over the head would probably kill him in his weakened condition. And if he came out of it too early, the shock certainly would kill him. This place is crawling with germs. We can't dunk it all in boiling water.'

Again Russ paused for thought, a frown inscribing deep lines into the skin of his grizzled features. Then the cunning glint appeared in his narrowed eyes. 'So I'll take him back to Kansas City. You I don't need any more.'

Jubal had remained fully dressed throughout the treatment, even to keeping his hat on. Now he tilted the derby on to the back of his head. He drew a hand across his forehead, wiping off the sweat. Perhaps the fire had oozed his pores; perhaps the nervous tension of removing the bullet; perhaps fear of Russ. More likely a combination of all three, he decided.

'You can start heading for Kansas City,' he replied at length. 'Day's ride if your brother doesn't slow you down.'

'Day and a half at the most,' Russ said.

'If he stays in the saddle,' Jubal came back. 'Could be he'll hold out against fever. Maybe that shattered lead won't start infecting his blood. He might not even pass out again.' Jubal held the valise towards Russ. 'But if anything like that happens, you'll find something in here to help.'

Fear, anger and confusion were combined in Russ's eyes. 'What you tryin' to pull, Cade?' he demanded.

Jubal seemed about to reply, but Russ cut in before he

could start.

'Okay. I wouldn't know what to do with any of the junk in that bag of tricks. So you ride to Kansas City with us.'

Jubal lowered the bag and shook his head slowly. 'Appreciate the offer, but not me. If I ride out of here, it's in the other direction. I'm heading for Cheyenne.'

A harsh laugh ripped from Russ's lips. 'You ain't in any position to argue, mister!' he snarled, anger winning over the other emotions that had been battling in his mind. 'I got this.'

He slapped the stock of the Winchester.

'That's a real killer of an argument,' Jubal answered softly, and half raised the valise again. 'But I've got this.' He crooked the index finger of his free hand and tapped the side of his head. 'And up here I've got the knowledge of how to use what's inside it.'

'That ain't no argument at all,' Russ retorted without conviction.

'I figure it's a life-saver,' Jubal countered, flicking his gaze towards Clarke as the injured man showed the first signs of returning consciousness.

Russ continued to glare fixedly at Jubal. For a long time the crackle of the fire was the only sound in the room. Then full awareness hit Clarke and he emitted a deep-throated groan of agony.

'All you win is an argument, Cade,' Russ surrendered. 'Buys you some time. Use it well – taking care of my brother.'

'Happy to take care of you both,' Jubal answered softly, and showed his broken-toothed grin openly for the first time since riding into the farmstead.

Russ read the obvious double meaning in the remark, made even more blatant by the grin. But another groan from Clarke warned him against hasty action. Frustrated rage burned inside him. The way he looked now it was impossible to imagine the kind of respect he had shown while watching Jubal at work. And Jubal knew he had pushed the man to the limit – another fraction of an inch and brotherly affection would be ignored: brushed aside with every other consideration by the urge to kill.

'Russ, he's cut my friggin' arm off!' Clark shrieked, swinging his good arm across his body to feel for the one which numbness seemed to make disappear.

'Should have been your damn tongue!' Russ snarled a moment before compassion for his brother's anguish swept away the misdirected anger. His voice and expression softened. 'It's okay, Clarke. You're gonna be okay.'

He stooped down beside the injured man, but tilted his head to look up at Jubal. His eyes made a demand, moderated to a request, for confirmation. Clarke needed to force nothing. The tacit plea written across his pain twisted face was a genuine appeal.

'You'll pull through,' he supplied softly. Then added: 'With care.'

CHAPTER SEVEN

Because he knew that, for a time, any attempt to undermine the authority of Russ Longstreet's Winchester would be unnecessarily dangerous, Jubal fixed breakfast. Since he was urgently in need of a hot meal himself it was no hardship to treble the quantities of salted pork, beans, grits and coffee. Clarke slept fitfully until the meal was ready while Russ returned to his position against the door. Cold sunlight shafted through the few remaining window panes and icy draughts trickled through cracks and holes in the walls. But it stayed comfortably warm inside for Jubal did not allow the fire to die down. When the kindling from the smashed crates was exhausted, he tore up floorboards from the bedroom and added these to the flames.

Russ gently awoke his brother when breakfast was ready. Clarke's shoulder was immovably stiff and Jubal had to help him to sit up and lean his back against the wall. They began the meal in silence.

'How did your buddy get ahead of you?' Jubal asked when all three had placated the initial pangs of hunger and their eating slowed down.

Clarke, deathly pale under the stubble and dirt of his face, clamped his lips tight closed and shot a glance across the room at Russ.

Russ finished chewing on a piece of pork before answering. His tone was sour. 'If he was still our buddy, I wouldn't let him lay out there in the yard, Cade. Clarke and me figured he'd just run out on us. But he tried to shaft us, looks like.'

'He seemed pretty happy to see you,' Jubal pointed out.

Russ sniffed loudly, then ran his cuff across his upper lip. 'Figured you had the beatin' of him, I reckon. Figured to tell us it was all a plan and he was only doin' his job.' It

81

could be nothing but a theory and Russ gave the impression that he didn't care one way or the other. He was just talking for the sake of it.

'He must have thought there really was —'

'Shut up!' Russ roared at his brother.

Clarke clamped his lips together again and flattened his back against the wall. He winced as the shoulder wound exploded with pain. Jubal looked from the pained and frightened face of one man to the cold fury inscribed on the features of the other. Then, in the tense silence, he drank his coffee and had to make an effort not to hazard guesses about the unspoken end of Clarke's remark. He would either find out for certain what the injured man intended to say, or he would not. Meantime he had to rely on known facts to deal with his present circumstances. And with hunger satisfied, rest for himself and care of his horse were the next priorities.

Russ came stiffly erect from his relaxed leaning against the door as Jubal rose.

'Horse needs feeding,' he explained evenly. 'Then I aim to sleep until noon.' He jerked on the gold chain stretched across his chest and hooked out a watch. He flipped open the lid. 'Six hours is enough for any man.'

Russ shook his head. 'We ride now. You're the one said Clarke needs more than he can get here.'

Clarke was recovering from the snap of Russ's anger. Now new fear leapt into his pained eyes. 'He said that?'

Jubal sighed. 'I'm betting he didn't get any sleep last night. I know he got shot this morning. He needs rest the most.'

Russ maintained his resolute pose for a few seconds more, then stepped to the side to allow Jubal passage to the door. 'You think you know it all, don't you, Cade?' he rasped churlishly.

'If I did I wouldn't be standing on the wrong end of a Winchester,' Jubal replied lightly, and went out into the icily cold, eerily still air of morning.

He heard Russ's footfalls behind him. Then his voice: 'Take care of our nags, too. They ain't had no more sleep than

82

Clarke and me.'

Jubal unhitched the two geldings and led them across the yard and into the barn. There he unsaddled them before walking all three horses over to the far side of the shack where the grass grew lush under the bluff. Russ stayed within ten feet of Jubal the whole time, the Winchester always levelled on target. The horses were allowed fifteen minutes to graze before being led to the edge of the stream. Then they were returned to the barn. The men exchanged no more conversation after Russ had given his curt instruction.

When they re-entered the shack Clarke was stretched out on the blankets again, snoring softly. Jubal took off his topcoat, sat down against the wall near the fire and draped the coat over him, back to front. He tilted the derby forward so that the brim shaded his eyes from the sunlight.

'You might as well sleep, Cade,' Russ said coldly. 'Either Clarke or me'll be awake the whole time.'

'Appreciate it if you don't make too much noise changing guard,' Jubal replied.

Russ Longstreet's voice had sounded distant. His own words seemed to come from even farther away. Tension fused with simple weariness to enlarge to exhaustion. Within moments he was in a deep sleep. A rifle shot shattered the dark luxury and he came awake smelling the acrid odour of fire ash. He snapped open his eyes and tilted up his hat brim to see Russ in his familiar position at the door. The Winchester was trailing smoke from its muzzle and a billow of grey ash was re-settling in the grate after the bullet had raised it.

'Sun ain't gonna get no higher, Cade,' the elder Longstreet said.

The light shafting through the unbroken panes was brighter. But the draughts were a lot colder with no fire to combat them. Clarke was on his feet close to one of the windows, fully dressed. His face had more colour now and was less haggard.

'Tell him how you feel, Clarke,' Russ said with a bitter grin as Jubal stood up and shrugged into his topcoat.

'Better, doc,' Clarke reported happily. 'Not good, but better. You fixed me up fine.'

'So who needs you, Cade?' Ross asked softly. The action of the Winchester sounded very loud.

Jubal held Russ's evil gaze and kept his tone light: 'You want to ask me again after we've ridden the first three or four hundred feet?'

Clarke's good mood disintegrated and he raised a hand to the bulge at his injured shoulder. 'Russ, don't do nothin' hasty now. What trouble's he gonna be for a while? If things work out, we can blast him later.'

Russ nodded at once, without taking time to think about it. 'Okay, Cade. You get to stay alive – for a while.'

'Appreciate that,' Jubal replied evenly, stooping to hoist up his gear.

Russ opened the door and Jubal led the way across the yard. Clarke discovered how weak he was on the short journey and when they reached the barn Jubal concealed his satisfaction at the look of concern on Russ's face. Jubal saddled the stallion and strapped on his refolded bedroll while Russ attended to the other two horses. Clarke held the Winchester on Jubal, gripping it one-handed and squatting down to rest the barrel across his knees.

'My rifle's out by the trees, Russ,' he said when they were ready to mount.

'Watch him close, Clarke,' the elder brother warned.

'There's a Spencer out there, too,' Jubal called as Russ started for the door. 'It's got sentimental value.'

This was true. The carbine had been bequeathed to Jubal by the only friend he had made in the Chicago foundling home where they were both raised. The friend had been killed during one of the final battles of the War Between the States. A London gunsmith had made the conversion from carbine to rifle barrel and since then Jubal had always kept the old Spencer close by him.

'I ain't one for sentiment,' Russ rasped. 'Specially when it could get me killed.'

'Didn't think you'd let me carry it,' Jubal replied. 'But unless one of you brings it along, my time's run out. Clarke will have a little longer.'

Rage threatened to well up in Russ again.

'Get it for him, please,' Clarke implored.

'You don't want that toy iron as well?' Russ asked with heavy sarcasm.

'Ain't no toy,' Clarke muttered, pained. 'I oughta know that.'

'I'm not sentimental about poker,' Jubal replied. He had won the Remington under-and-over in a game of stud with some fellow medical students in London.

The meaning of his comment was, of course, lost on both men. Russ strode angrily out of the barn and Clarke showed puzzlement for a few moments. Then his concern about Jubal's constant warnings took over his mind.

'My shoulder really as bad as you're makin' out, doc?' he whined.

'Shut up, Clarke!' Russ bellowed from beyond the side wall of the barn.

'Your problems aren't only physical,' Jubal replied softly.

Clarke's voice was a low whisper. 'What's that supposed to mean?'

'Reckon you're repressed,' Jubal answered.

Clarke blinked, confused. 'That don't tell me nothin', doc,' he whispered.

'Makes us even,' Jubal said.

Clarke held a miserable silence until his brother returned, carrying the Winchester and the Spencer. He thrust both rifles into the bedroll slung behind Clarke's saddle. Jubal saw that his gun had an ugly scar gouged along the stock. Russ retrieved his own rifle and helped Clarke back on to his feet.

'Boost him into the saddle, Cade,' the elder brother instructed. 'Touch one of them rifles and he'll have to take his chances.'

'Thanks a whole friggin' bunch, Russ,' Clarke said wryly, moving to his horse.

Jubal helped him up into the saddle, uncomfortably aware of the Winchester trained on his back. The rifle jerked in a tacit order to mount the stallion and ride out of the barn. Then Russ mounted and the two brothers moved in Jubal's wake. Death and the biting cold seemed to make the stiff corpse of Ron Fairchild as one with the iron hard ground across which he was sprawled.

'He got what was comin' to him,' Russ growled, then sniffed and cuffed his upper lip.

'For trying to double-cross the boss like that,' Clarke augmented, then was driven into sullen, tight-lipped silence by a withering look from his brother.

Jubal tugged on the reins to turn the stallion west, towards the stand of timber.

'What the hell's that way,' Russ asked disgruntled, but turning his horse to follow. 'Cepting for wild country and dirt farms like this. Most of them without anybody living there no more, like here.'

'Way out there is Cheyenne,' Jubal answered without turning around as he urged the stallion in among the trees.

'That's a dream you won't live to see, Cade,' Russ answered coldly. 'And even if you make it, won't have nothin' like like Kansas City for takin' care of sick people.'

Now it was Jubal's turn to force silence on the group by not responding. Talk was useless now that he had achieved his initial objective of heading in the right direction, with both brothers convinced Clarke was in a bad way. Hard riding and Clarke's gullibility and tendency towards malingering self-pity would support the lie for as long as he was kept away from a second medical opinion. And with each minute that ticked away, the circumstances would be marginally changed. So Jubal was prepared to await the right circumstance before making his move: the one in which he would have the greatest chance of getting the drop on the Longstreets with the lowest risk to himself. With his responsibility towards Andy Prescott and his dead wife. Jubal did not consider himself guilty of being over-cautious.

The timber stretched for almost two miles and it was all hard going through the thick tangle of brush. The verbal silence was broken only once, by Clarke speaking through teeth clenched against pain.

'Remember what we heard in Kansas City, Russ,' he rasped. 'Bunch of renegade Sioux out there. Given the bum's rush south by their own people. Long way from home and mean with it.'

Russ had responded with a non-committal grunt and no other words were spoken until Jubal led the way clear on the far side of the timber. Flat, monotonous, tall-grass prairie rolled away to seeming infinity in front of them. To the south the view was precisely the same. But in the far north the horizon was marked by the rise of a line of hills.

'Ain't nothin' out there gonna help Clarke,' Russ growled.

'Except me,' Jubal answered, heeling his horse forward on a course towards the north-west. He glanced over his shoulder and saw that Russ was scowling. Clarke's face was set in a permanent grimace, devoid of colour again from the weakening, pain-arousing struggle through the timber. He was staring straight ahead through eyes that seemed hollow, sitting tight to the saddle so that his body jarred with each step taken by his gelding.

They were two hours out into the grass when he reined his horse to a halt and croaked 'Hell, I gotta rest.'

Jubal halted his own mount and slid from the saddle without waiting for Russ to give the command. It was conceivable that Clarke had picked up an infection which could make his wound fatal. And with the younger brother dead, Jubal had nothing with which to bargain against the elder Longstreet's urge to kill him.

'A fire for some hot water and food,' Jubal demanded as he helped Clarke to dismount.

Aware that Jubal was once more an earnest doctor before he was a reluctant captive, Russ put up no argument. As Jubal bared the wound by opening Clarke's clothes and removing the dressing, Russ built a grass fire. It was hard work

– first clearing a site and then constantly feeding more fast-burning fuel to the flames. Jubal remained intent upon his task. The jolting Clarke had taken had oozed fresh blood, but it was a clean and bright red and there was no surface sign of infection. He washed the bullet hole and applied more salve. Fleetingly, he thought of rubbing a little dirt in the wound, but he dismissed the idea at once. And not for fear of being seen. A natural instinct born in him? Or something instilled in him by the solemn swearing of the Hippocratic Oath? It was immaterial. Given a gun in his hand, he could willingly have put a bullet through the head of the helpless Clarke Longstreet. But to cold-bloodedly misuse his hard-learned skills to achieve the same end – this was something he could not do.

They rested for an hour and ate a meagre meal of boiled jerked beef. Then the cold and the tiring effort of maintaining the fire drove them forward again. The sun remained tantalizingly bright in a cloudless sky as the temperature stayed just above freezing. After nightfall, it did freeze and they made camp in a small hollow where brush supplied wood for a fire. Because of the two against one situation Jubal was again allowed an uninterrupted sleep while the Longstreets took turns at standing guard and keeping the fire bright.

During the afternoon, Clarke had grown weaker. The sporadic periods of sleep during the night went some way to refreshing him but as they set off again across the frost-laden prairie it was obvious that the pain and self-pity would continue to erode his already low morale. At the third stop of the morning when the sun was as bright and the air as cold as yesterday, Russ ended a long period of deep thought.

'I figure you're stallin', Cade,' he said quietly on a stream of cigarette smoke.

'You do?' Jubal asked in the same easy tone.

'It's the travellin' that's makin' Clarke feel so bad. I figure ain't nothin' wrong with his shoulder that wouldn't heal up by just restin' it.'

Clarke came out of his taciturn misery to show interest.

88

'You reckon, Russ?'

They had lit no fire this stop. Clarke was sitting down, hugging his knees to his chest with his good arm. Jubal and Russ were standing.

'I'm calling you,' Jubal said, casting a glance around him and settling his gaze on the hills. They were much closer today. Less than three hours of easy riding away, he assessed. 'It's a bluff and you're just guessing what I'm holding. But even if you've guessed right, he'd need more than a couple of hours' rest. Couple of days at least. Maybe more than a week.' He swung around to gaze fixedly at Russ. 'But neither of you would last that long out here. Be a toss-up whether starvation or exposure would kill you first.'

Both Longstreets remained silent for a long time. Then it was Clarke who spoke, from out of his well of misery again as he struggled to his feet.

'Damn right, Russ! We gotta get to some kind of shelter and we ain't got grub for more than a day.' He looked towards the hills that had held Jubal's interest. 'There just has to be a town or somethin' up there.'

'Cade?' Russ said.

'You calling?' Jubal asked.

'Just want you to know. When you die, it'll be the hard way. And I mean slow. I hate smart guys.'

He swung up into the saddle and waited impatiently for the others to mount. They set off again with Jubal, as always, riding at the front so that he was covered by Russ's Winchester. Periodically, as they drew closer to the hills, he heard the elder Longstreet talking urgently to his brother. From the occasional word he picked up distinctly it was obvious Russ was encouraging Clarke to stay in the saddle and not give in to the pain and exhaustion.

The Sioux hit them as they rode into a valley at the edge of the rising ground.

CHAPTER EIGHT

There were between twenty and thirty braves, all mounted on ponies. They attacked as a single group, cresting the brow of a hill on the white men's left. For long seconds they held their silence, looking down the long incline towards the slow-moving trio of riders below. Then the sub-chief who was their leader emitted a terrifying war-cry and heeled his pony forward. The braves shrieked their delight and streamed after him.

The Longstreets and Jubal snapped their heads around and saw the attackers, descending upon them at a full gallop. The Sioux wore headbands but no feathers. Long black hair streamed out behind burnished, dark-eyed faces daubed with white paint. Lithe bodies canted forward, clothed in long-sleeved buck-skin tunics. Moccasined feet thudded into the flanks of the ponies. Legginged knees gripped horseflesh while the braves used their hands to fit arrows into bows.

'The bastard renegades!' Clarke yelled, his pain suddenly of secondary importance.

Jubal was the first to demand a gallop from his horse. Clarke was hard behind him and Russ raced up at the rear after sending a shot towards the braves. The bullet had the range but momentary panic misdirected it. One over-excited brave let loose an arrow, but it fell far short of the target. Jubal had no weapon and since Clarke had to use his good hand to keep a grip on the reins, he was unable to draw his Remington. Russ concentrated upon racing away from the Indians without thought of discouraging them after the single shot.

The braves changed course on the slope, veering towards the fleeing white men and increasing the volume of their war-cries. Jubal maintained his lead over the Longstreets, galloping the stallion at full stretch along the bottom of the valley. Ahead, it narrowed to a rocky gorge which seemed to be blocked by a cliff-face. But the valley had become too steep-sided to offer an alternative means of escape. He rode into the gorge as a clutch of arrows bounced off the rocks at his side. The Longstreets were only moments behind him, Clarke screaming in terror as an arrow thudded into the bed-roll behind his saddle. The new steepness of the ground on either side concentrated the whoops and cries of the Sioux, the extra volume investing them with an even more terrifying quality.

The gorge was not blocked. Instead, it made a sharp, almost right angled turn. The fast-running water of a stream splashed beneath the thudding hooves of the three horses. The narrow-ness of the gorge – it allowed no more than four men to ride abreast – caused the braves to slow their headlong pursuit as they crowded in through the entrance. The white men contin-ued to urge their horses to the limit, racing around a long curve that swung them northwards.

Ahead of him, as the turn in the gorge diminished the sound of the Sioux' excitement, Jubal saw a chance of escape. A slim one, but better than trying to outrun a numerically stronger enemy who were probably riding fresher horses. Fifty yards ahead the gorge widened into a broad area of hollows and rises liberally scattered with boulders from a primeval landslip. All around were rock- and earth-faced cliffs showing the ancient scars of being torn apart. To attempt to gallop a horse across such terrain would be inviting a fall: and the animal would be lucky to survive without at least a broken leg.

Jubal snatched a glance over his shoulder and saw the Long-streets galloping less than six feet behind him: side by side, with Russ holding Clarke in the saddle by gripping the scruff of his neck. The bend in the gorge continued to hide the Sioux. But the nearness of the braves was made clear by their whooping and hollering.

Timing his move precisely, Jubal veered the stallion to the right and jerked hard on the reins. The animal came out of the headlong gallop and started to rear at the edge of the broken ground. Jubal kicked free of the stirrups, released the reins and grabbed the saddlebags. Russ Longstreet yelled something at him but Jubal didn't hear it as he swung his right leg across the neck of the rearing stallion. For a split second he was seated side-saddle. Then he was clear of the snorting animal, bending his knees for the impact with the rocky bed of the shallow stream. The geldings with the Longstreets astride them, flashed across in front of Jubal. He reached out his free hand, felt a rifle stock and jerked at it. He hit the streambed and fell forward, the flying rear hooves of Clarke's horse narrowly missing his head.

It felt as if every bone in his body was shattered by the impact and for a seeming eternity he screwed his eyes tight shut and was afraid to try moving. But this fear, in fact, lasted only a second as the war-cries of the Sioux braves beat against his ears. He opened his eyes and saw it was his own Spencer rifle he had drawn from the bedroll. The icy bite of the water numbed his pain and he struggled upright, whirling around. His head moved so fast that all he saw was a blur of rugged rocks and crumbled earth. The water of the stream reflected the sunlight with dazzling brilliance. He had to will himself into a staggering run, away from the mouth of the gorge towards a craggy heap of grotesquely weathered boulders. As soon as he was in among them, he flung himself to the ground and allowed a tide of pain to sweep up from his ankles and engulf his entire body.

But the rising sound of the approaching Sioux attackers urged him up on to all fours: to check that he was in cover and to survey the chances of his hiding place being discovered. The pile of boulders did, in fact, give him adequate cover for the moment: and enabled him to see a large area of the terrain beyond. He was in time to see the Longstreets disappear over the crest of a low rise in the wake of the riderless stallion. Then he swung his gaze back to the mouth of the gorge just as the leading bunch of braves appeared, skidding their ponies to a halt. Their blood-curdling screams died on their lips and their eyes flashed with anger as they stared out across the apparently deserted area of broken ground.

The sub-chief shouted an order back into the gorge and the braves at the rear halted their ponies and became silent. But the quiet was not absolute. The unmistakable sound of shod horses moving at a gallop trembled in the still air. A brave yelled and raised an arm to point. Jubal swung his head to look in the same direction as the Indians and gave a non-committal grunt as the stallion and two geldings raced up out of the dip. All three horses were now riderless. They galloped away, sometimes in sight and sometimes not. But the sound of their thudding hooves was lost several seconds before the horses disappeared through a cleft in a cliff-face.

Jubal looked back towards the Indians just as the sub-chief began to issue orders for a search pattern, supplementing his words with energetic hand gestures. The braves listened intently, then spread out in a long line. They moved their horses forward slowly, controlling the animals with their knees as they held an arrow in each bow, string pulled taut. Jubal was directly in line with the right flank of the advance and only ten yards from its starting point. Close enough to see every detail of the face and clothing of the nearest brave: and to see that his appearance matched that of all the others.

Young enough to be a hot-head, and suffering the consequences of recklessness. There was no way of knowing how long the renegades had been cast out from their tribe and forced to survive in hostile territory. But a long time, it seemed. They were emaciated by malnutrition and at least a third of them had open sores or scabs showing through the grime and paint on their faces. Their clothing was filthy and torn, telling of many weeks without attention from the squaws, while not a single brave was armed with anything except the traditional weapons of bows, knives and tomahawks. But against such weaknesses had to be set the fact that there were thirty braves. And Jubal was on his own – he disregarded the possibility of help from the Longstreets because there were too many variables.

The respite between hurling his aching body among the boulders and the start of the Indians' slow advance had been short. But at least it had enabled Jubal to isolate the pain to his lower legs so that the reflexes elsewhere in his body felt unimpaired. He was stretched out full-length, looking along the line of advance through a triangle between two boulders wedged together. There was just enough clearance in the aperture to allow him to draw a bead upon any of the twenty braves farthest from him. Those closer to him were protected by the rocks in front and to the side of him. But although he could not see them, he was aware that these braves would be the first to spot him as they moved over or around the rocks.

City bred and long out of the country, these Indians were the first Jubal had ever seen in his life. But he had read a great deal about them – along with every other aspect of life in the American West – in books he had consumed avidly whenever there was spare time from his studies in London. It was from such reading that he had nurtured his dream of practising medicine in the frontier country instead of the more lucrative cities. A dream that was now as dead as Mary.

Various books had put forward contradictory facts and theories regarding many things. Now, as he raked the aim of the Spencer along the line of slow-moving, raddle-faced Sioux braves he recalled one alleged fact purported in some books and ridiculed in others: that if you killed the leader of an Indian band, his followers would lose their will to fight and run scared. He drew a bead on the sub-chief and put the theory to the test.

The shot cracked with the utmost clarity against the steady shuffle of unshod hooves. For a split-second the world stood still: ponies and riders seemed like frozen images, as unmoving as the ground supporting them. Then a great gout of blood gushed from the side of the sub-chief's head, splashing over the brave riding on one side of him. The brave shrieked in horror. The sub-chief toppled from his pony, crashing down across the back of the next animal in line. This pony reared, tossing his rider clear, and bolted. The sub-chief's pony took off in pursuit.

Abruptly, the world was in a turmoil as the line of advance exploded into movement. With raised voices screaming in anger or fear, the braves broke in every direction. Some charged forward, others veered to the sides while still more wheeled their ponies for flight. A few slid from their animals and raced for cover on foot.

Jubal saw all this in a flash as he peered through the aperture between the rocks. Then he withdrew the Spencer and hurled himself over on to his back. For a moment, the sun dazzled him. The next moment it was blotted out, except for a bright aura that seemed to emanate from the brave who had leapt from his pony on to a boulder. Jubal had pumped a fresh shell into the breech as he rolled. Now he fired, an instant before the brave let loose his arrow. Blood exploded from the Indian's chest and showered over Jubal. The arrow buried its head deep in the ground at his side. The brave screamed as the impact of the bullet flung him backwards off the boulder.

The desperate desire for survival subjugated the pain in Jubal's legs as he scrambled to his feet, sitting low on his haunches. A high-pitched war-cry warned him of a new attack and he whirled around, working the action of the Spencer. A brave had raced around the boulders on his pony and was bearing down on Jubal. He loosed an arrow and Jubal fell to the side, firing as he did so. The pony tossed up his head and stopped the bullet. His forelegs collapsed first and his rider was pitched forward. The brave landed sure-footed in a head-long run, hurling away his bow and drawing a tomahawk. Jubal knew he did not have the time to cock and fire the rifle. The brave hurled himself forward for the kill. Jubal half rose to meet the attack and made a vicious jab with the Spencer. The muzzle rammed into the Indian's groin and his cry of triumph became a scream of agony. Jubal used his victim's momentum as he flung himself back against the ground and raised the rifle in a pitchfork action. The howling brave was lifted into the air on the barrel of the Spencer then hurled over Jubal's prostrate body. He smashed head-first into a boulder, his skull bursting open to pour out his brains. The tomahawk dropped on to Jubal's stomach, flat of the blade towards him.

He rolled clear of the falling, limp body of the brave and powered himself up into a crouch, jacking a shell into the breech. Two arrows hissed through the air and thudded into the carcase of the shot pony. Jubal whirled as twin cries of rage signalled the approach of a new attack. Two braves were galloping their ponies towards the boulders, both in the process of fitting fresh arrows into their bows. Jubal thrust himself up to his full height, smacking the scarred stock of the Spencer into his shoulder. Two snap shots sent both Indians clear of their mounts, blood streaming from their chests. The lead ripped into their hearts to bring instant, silent death. The loose ponies veered to the side and raced away. Their galloping hoofbeats were the only sounds trapped between the pitted cliff-faces surrounding the battlefield.

Jubal remained fully erect for compressed seconds, whirling first one way and then the other. Then he crouched and went forward to hunch against the boulders between which he had fired the first shot. He dug fresh shells from his jacket pocket and pushed them into the Spencer's magazine as he considered what his snap survey had shown. The great majority of the braves had regrouped at the mouth of the gorge. There had been no time to count them but he was sure not all of them had gathered in the shallow stream. For they were all mounted and there were at least ten riderless ponies running loose.

He made a mental tally and discovered he had killed five braves. But because this was the only fact he could be sure of, there was no way of knowing how many braves were hidden out there among the rock-strewn rises and dips. He also knew, of course, that the theory of killing the chief to finish the fight was not valid. Not as far as the Sioux were concerned, at least.

He completed the reloading and prepared to raise himself up for another fast surveillance of the area beyond his protective boulders. From the corner of his eye he caught sight of the pair of saddlebags, the one of them bulged by the package it contained. The simple act of electing to snatch the saddlebags rather than the valise seemed to crystallize his transformation from one kind of man to another who was totally different.

He rose and stared into the startled eyes of a brave straightening up on the other side of the boulder. The Indian was in the process of lifting his tomahawk. The Spencer was cocked and pointing. Jubal rested the barrel across the rock and squeezed the trigger. Because of the rifle's cant, the bullet tunnelled into the brave's throat. It went up through the roof of his mouth, twisted through his brain and exited in a shower of gore through the top of his skull. The dead man slammed down like a felled tree.

Jubal pumped the action of the rifle and remained standing, staring across the intervening ground at the cluster of mounted braves in the mouth of the gorge. The Indians were motionless, hatred blazing in every pair of dark eyes. But there was something impotent about the braves, as if they were powerless to vent their fury without a triggering act to release it. But it wasn't that at all.

'Behind you!' Russ Longstreet screamed.

Jubal saw every brave's head swing, their anger draining under an onslaught of fear as they sought to identify a new enemy. Then he turned himself, in a whirling crouch that took him under the flight of a hissing arrow. The Spencer cracked and another brave died. He was less than ten feet away from Jubal and the bullet exploded through his jugular vein just as he was reaching over his shoulder to draw another arrow from his pouch. His dying scream became a gurgle as blood swamped his throat. It was the sight of one of their number creeping up on Jubal from the rear which had held the other braves motionless in a burning rage of frustration.

When Jubal swung around again to look towards them the

Sioux had split into two groups and each brave had an arrow slotted against a taut bowstring. There was a full-throated shout and two showers of arrows were hissed through the air. Jubal ducked and pressed himself hard against the boulders as more than a dozen feathered shafts arced towards him. Another clutch of arrows zoomed into the dip where the Longstreet brothers were concealed.

Shafts snapped against the boulders and thudded into the ground: some penetrated the dead flesh of the pony and one of the braves behind Jubal. Expecting a charge with war whoops and a further hail of deadly missiles, Jubal tensed himself.

'They're friggin' beatin' it!' Clarke Longstreet yelled in delight.

Jubal bobbed up, then down again as arrows hissed towards his hiding place. But he saw enough to apparently confirm Clarke's news. The arrows were being loosed as covering fire for three braves who had been hiding among the boulders. While the mounted braves kept the white men pinned down, the three were running full tilt for the mouth of the gorge. Jubal stretched himself out full-length beside the boulders and peered through the aperture at the base. New arrows were already slotted and aimed. But they were not released; for the breathless runners had reached safety.

There was an excited babble of conversation as the three who had abandoned their ponies swung up to ride tandem on other mounts. Then the whole group wheeled and set off into the gorge at a gallop, spray flying from pumping hooves. They rode around the bend and the clatter of their progress diminished and faded completely.

'Cade?' Russ Longstreet called.

Jubal got slowly and carefully to his feet and scanned the terrain in every direction, the barrel of the Spencer swinging at the same rate as he turned. The only Indians in sight were those sprawled in the stillness of death.

'I'm here!' he shouted when he had completed one turn and started on another.

'Could be a trick,' the elder Longstreet called. 'They know there's only three of us.'

There was a dip in the ground twenty yards to the right of where Jubal had made his stand. As he completed the second turn, he lunged away from the boulders and raced for the dip. He reached the fresh cover safely and from there could no longer see the corpses. The sun shone bright and the stream gurgled happily. It was a very peaceful scene.

'They also know at least one of us has got a rifle,' Jubal called, sprinting for a large, almost cube-shaped chunk of rock. The distance was greater this time and the result was the same. He felt certain no sharpshooters had been left hiding in the area.

'Didn't get no chance at a clear shot,' Russ excused.

'I'm bleedin' like a stuck pig again, doc,' Clarke whined. 'From when I jumped clear of the nag.'

'Not making house calls right now,' Jubal replied wryly, no longer having to shout.

He was now level with the brothers' hiding place and less than twenty feet away from it. When he moved out into the open, he did not run. Instead, he hobbled, now fully aware of the sharp pain extending from ankles to knees in both legs. He was also aware that he was carrying the saddlebags over his shoulder, although he could not remember picking them up.

'Hey, Cade?'

Jubal halted and looked back over his shoulder. The Longstreets were emerging from the dip, Russ supporting the sagging form of his brother. He carried the Winchester in his free hand but because of his burden the gun no longer offered a threat to Jubal.

'Give me a hand with Clarke, will you?'

Jubal split his lips to show the broken-toothed grin. His dark eyes glinted with a frosty light and on the background of his stubbled features the expression bore the stamp of evil. 'One of us has gone crazy, and it's not me, Longstreet,' he rasped.

99

Anger flared across the elder brother's face but he killed it immediately. 'At least wait for us,' he growled, trying to move faster.

But Clarke was almost a dead-weight, head lolling down on to his chest and feet dragging. Jubal waited, trying to ignore his own pain.

'Keep moving,' he said when the men drew level with him. He held the Spencer low and one-handed, presenting no threat. But his quietly authoritative tone demanded compliance.

'You got even less to worry about from me now, Cade,' Russ said as he continued to struggle along with Clarke in tow. 'He needs you more than ever. And I ain't about to blast a white man while there's Sioux close by. You did all right back there, mister.'

Jubal was hobbling along in the wake of the Longstreets, heading for the cleft in the cliff face through which their horses had disappeared. Russ did not look around as he spoke, so Jubal was unable to see the man's face. But he detected in the voice a kind of grudging respect as the compliment was paid. He did not reply.

'You turned plenty of them bastards into good Indians. Scared the crap outta the rest of 'em.'

They drew close to where a Sioux pony was grazing on a grassy patch at the bank of the stream. Jubal made a lunge, reaching for the rope bridle. But the pony gave a snort and backed away. Jubal made another try and the animal turned and bolted.

'Not a hope in hell's chance of catchin' one of 'em,' Russ said wearily. 'Damn ponies are sneakier than the bastards that ride 'em.'

He sniffed and drew his cuff across his upper lip as he dragged his brother through the split in the cliff-face. It sliced through the great slab of rock like a gigantic knife-cut. The high sides kept out sunlight and the air was damp and chillingly cold. Breathing it revived Clarke and he returned to awareness with a deep-throated groan of pain.

100

'I'm dyin', Russ,' he whined. 'God, my shoulder's killin' me.'

'Cade'll take a look at it soon as we find a place to rest up, kid,' Russ replied soothingly.

Clarke raised his chin up from his chest and forced strength into his legs. He planted his feet down firmly, stopping dead and forcing his brother to halt.

'The bastard ain't here no more!' he yelled in terror.

'Where the hell would he go?' Russ barked, his mood back to normal again.

Clarke snapped his head around and a smile of relief shone through the grimace of pain when he saw Jubal standing behind him. But then hopelessness became the dominant expression. 'Where's your bag of stuff?' he whined.

'Had to make a choice,' Jubal replied evenly and patted the bulging saddlebag. 'Figured this was the more important.'

Clarke's body sagged again as he turned and started forward. 'Doc, did you make a mistake,' he muttered. 'Ain't nothin' —'

'Shut up, Clarke!' Russ snarled.

Jubal hobbled after the brothers as they moved towards the end of the cleft through the rock, marked by a wedge of bright sunlight. When they reached it, Russ was the one to force an abrupt halt. Clarke snapped up his head to see what had caused the sudden decision.

'Will you look at that?' the elder brother hissed with subdued joy.

'If I knew I wasn't meant for hell, I'd figure I was dead,' Clarke put in, his tone matching that of Russ. 'That sure is heaven.'

Jubal moved up close behind them and looked between their heads. The ground fell away sharply and then levelled out for a grass-carpeted strip about a quarter of a mile wide with thick timber on the far side. Lumbering along the centre of the wide, natural trail was a train of ten covered wagons. As many outriders formed an alert escort, jogging along with rifles drawn and resting across their saddlehorns.

101

'Expecting trouble, looks like,' Russ said, the moment of low-keyed enthusiasm over.

'So let's go and give them the benefit of our experience,' Jubal said evenly.

CHAPTER NINE

They started down the incline which was mostly bare rock with just the occasional pocket of earth supporting tangled brush. The drop was steep enough to give Jubal trouble. The Longstreets – one very weak and the other drained by the effort of carrying the burden – had to constantly struggle against the force of gravity which tugged at their clinging forms. After a while, Jubal moved on ahead of them and he was halfway to the bottom when a single shout, followed by several more, signalled that their approach had been spotted The wagons rolled to a halt and the outriders converged into a group opposite the point where Jubal would reach level ground. He was very conscious of being scrutinized with massed suspicion as he descended the final few feet.

The climb down had increased the ache in the bruised muscles of his legs and he halted gratefully, pressing the stock of the Spencer into the ground and leaning on it. He looked across at the group of horsemen and saw that they spanned a broad age gap, from late twenties to sixty-plus. Behind them on the stalled wagons, women from young to old held the reins on the teams. And a few children poked their heads out from canvas flaps. Three spare horses were hitched to the tailgate of the lead wagon and Jubal recognized them with a jolt of surprise: closely followed by a surge of elation when he saw the valise was still firmly secured to the stallion's saddle.

The Longstreets struggled down off the incline and halted beside Jubal. Russ stood panting for a short while, then gently stooped to lower his brother to the ground. Clarke's breathing was ragged and his eyes were closed in his haggard, ghastly grey face. A large bloodstain was spread across his shoulder.

The horsemen walked their animals towards the travel and

battle-weary trio.

'They ain't gonna just ignore us then,' Russ growled between taking deep breaths.

'Just hope they don't rate our horses as more important than us,' Jubal replied.

Russ raked his exhausted gaze along the line of wagons and gave a grunt of satisfaction when he saw the two geldings and the stallion. 'So we ain't gonna ask for no help,' he murmured as the men from the train closed in. 'Just for what's ours. Being beholden ain't my style.'

He said this loud enough for the riders to hear, but it was obviously meant as much for Jubal as them. The men from the train halted, rifles still resting across saddlehorns: making no threat but ready for instant use.

'You the three that lost the horses?' The speaker was big and broad-shouldered: about fifty with long blond hair and eyes that looked capable of staring into a man's mind. He had a European accent.

'That's us, mister,' Russ answered. 'But we didn't just lose 'em from being careless.'

'Trouble, uh? Mind telling us what kind?'

'Indian kind.'

The horsemen were not shocked. Just made more apprehensive. Several glanced nervously up the slope towards the sheer cliff-face at the top.

'They got him, uh?' the big blond asked, nodding towards the crumpled form of Clarke.

'Yeah,' Russ replied quickly, shooting a glance at Jubal. 'And if you let us have our horses back, we can take care of him.'

The big man swung his penetrating gaze towards Jubal. 'You are the doctor?'

'Anyone on the train sick?' Jubal asked.

The man was surprised. 'No.'

Jubal nodded. 'Then I'm the doctor. All right if I get my horse?'

'Mine and Clarke's as well,' Russ added quickly.

The big man nodded. Not consenting: just a gesture that he understood. 'We would hope your medical skills would not be required,' he said to Jubal. 'But we have been warned to expect an Indian attack. Two extra guns would be welcome.'

'I've got business that's pressing hard,' Jubal answered. 'Wagons don't roll fast enough.'

'The injured man cannot ride,' the big blond pointed out. 'I will be happy to put my wagon at his disposal.'

One of the younger men cut in before Jubal or Russ could reply. He spoke fast in a foreign tongue. Northern European, Jubal guessed. Probably a Swede. The big blond listened patiently as the other men nodded. None of them had ever appeared friendly. Now they seemed almost hostile. Jubal sensed Russ becoming tense at his side: taking a firmer grip on the Winchester. The big blond remained silent for a few moments after the man had finished.

Then he sighed. 'My companions are of the opinion that help given reluctantly is not worth having. They also feel that there is distrust between you men. Even hatred. I agree with them. But still I offer you a degree of comfort for the injured one in return for your fire power. If you wish to refuse, then I will, of course, return your horses to you.'

'I'll take my horse,' Jubal replied.

'And Clarke's gotta stay close by Cade,' Russ said quickly.

'Then there is nothing more to be said,' the big blond responded, jerking at the reins to turn his mount.

The others followed his lead and they cantered away, remaining in a tight group for a while, then splitting up to resume their escorting positions ahead of, on the flanks and behind the train. The big blond rode to the rear of the lead wagon, unhitched the three horses and galloped back.

'Accept my apologies for examining the contents of the bag,' he said when Jubal had taken the reins of the stallion and Russ had a firm hold on the two geldings. 'It was how I knew one of you was a doctor.' He glanced down at Clarke, then injected scorn into his penetrating stare which he fixed upon Jubal. 'But no doctor I have ever known was like you.'

105

His voice was harsh with contempt.

He wheeled his horse and galloped away, giving a shout and a gesture that set the wagons rolling again.

'Havin' that rifle won't save you if Clarke dies,' Russ warned.

Jubal unhooked the valise and set it down, then checked that both his canteens were still full. Clarke was hovering on the border between unconsciousness and awareness. As Jubal began to fold back his clothing to get to the re-opened wound, the younger Longstreet raised his eyelids. A hint of relief showed through his pain.

'Thanks, doc,' he whispered.

Jubal treated him to a frail smile, then ignored him. Just as he ignored the enmity which Russ was generating towards him. And the memory of the big blond's contempt. He concentrated all his attention on the wound, which still showed no sign of infection. But he knew Clarke was not malingering any more. The agony of falling from a galloping horse must have driven the man close to the edge of insanity. Shock in combination with a vast loss of blood made him a very sick man. Working on the wound, stemming the blood, cleaning it with cold, unsterile water and fixing a new dressing in place, Jubal struggled to contain an inner conflict.

But when the treatment was finished, his mind unleashed a turmoil of opposite emotions that seethed and clawed at each other. Grabbing the saddlebags instead of the valise. The surge of joy upon seeing that the valise was not lost. Shooting Clarke Longstreet and then taking care of him. These memories thrust uppermost from his broiling mind, the quintessential factors that crystallized his anguished dilemma. A killer bent on vengeance at any price or a skilled doctor destined to ease the suffering of others? A man could not be both.

But still he refused to make the decision. As he rose from Clarke's side, he snatched up the Spencer and levelled it at the startled Russ.

'What the hell?' the elder Longstreet growled, staring into Jubal's coldly empty eyes and halting the impulse to bring

106

up his own rifle.

'There's nothing wrong with your brother that rest and keeping the wound clean won't cure,' Jubal announced coldly.

Anger made an ugly mask of the stubbled face. 'So I called it right,' Russ snarled.

'You figured it right,' Jubal answered. 'But you didn't have the guts to call. So I'm showing. Load him on his horse and catch up with the wagons. Keep him stretched out flat and make sure he stays warm.'

'And what'll you do if I —'

'I'll put a bullet in you,' Jubal cut in.

'And maybe have two problems instead of just the one?' Russ answered with a bright smile of confidence and suddenly his eyes were like those of the big blond – seeming able to look clear through into Jubal's mind.

Jubal shook his head. 'Fairchild wasn't a problem.'

The smile died and the eyes returned to normal perspective again. They saw just the outer shell of the man and recognized his willingness to kill. 'Seems like you win, Cade.'

'So let go of the rifle,' Jubal told him.

The Winchester clattered to the ground. Clarke's matching rifle still jutted from the bedroll, but Russ knew better than to make a try for it as he lifted his injured brother into the saddle. Clarke had heard every word spoken in the exchange but his attitude did not alter. If he felt anything at learning his true condition, he was too weak to express it. And he certainly had no strength to participate in any action Russ or Jubal might trigger.

Russ swung up into his own saddle and sat calmly waiting for the next order. Jubal moved forward, picked up the Winchester and thrust it into the bedroll with the other one.

'Your ticket to ride the wagon train,' Jubal said, backing away.

He fixed the saddlebags in place and mounted, keeping the Spencer ready but not levelled. Both Longstreets had holstered revolvers, but they wore their gunbelts under their top coats.

'On your way.'

Russ looked at him levelly, the corners of his lips turned up in the ghost of another smile. 'Can you make it, Clarke?' he asked.

Clarke nodded. Russ heeled his gelding forward in a walk and Clarke fell in behind him. The injured brother tried to look back over his shoulder. But he swayed dangerously and decided against the move. Jubal stayed where he was, features set in the unmoving lines of a cold frown. Although Clarke's weakness forced a slow pace, the two riders gradually closed with the wagon train. And, when their approach was seen, the big blond called a halt to wait for them. The meeting took place better than half a mile from where Jubal sat astride the stallion. But as he watched the distant activity involved in loading Clarke aboard a wagon, Jubal could sense the tacit contempt being directed at him across the intervening grassland.

Then, as he thrust the Spencer into the boot and heeled the stallion forward, he dismissed the notion. For it mattered not at all what others thought of him.

He stayed on a course close at the foot of the steep incline while the train, as the wagons rolled again, held to a route midway between the hills and the trees. When he overhauled the west-bound immigrants he saw that Russ Longstreet had taken a place among the guards and was again armed with the Winchester. He knew the elder brother would not be prepared to leave things as they were. He and Clarke had ridden hard and long on the trail of the money: to steal it and kill the courier. There had always been a nagging suspicion in Jubal's mind that the latter aim had been the most important: and with each mile they had travelled together the contents of the saddlebag had appeared to mean less to the Longstreets.

But Jubal had always chosen to push aside the temptation to ponder the meaning of the brothers' attitude, which had been emphasized by the efforts Russ made to keep Clarke from talking about the package of money. Now, urging more speed from the stallion to canter ahead of the trundling wagons –

moving out of range of Russ's Winchester – Jubal again refused to speculate. The run-in with the Longstreets had slowed him down considerably and he had a great deal of time to make up. It was enough to know that, given the chance, Russ would kill him. The motivation did not matter.

The ground began to rise and the grass became tougher, then more thinly spread. Finally vegetation disappeared altogether and the stallion's hooves clattered on rock. But the natural trail continued to follow an almost straight line through the hills. The sun dipped towards and then touched the horizon ahead and the still air was at once even colder than it had been all day. Hunger gnawed at Jubal's stomach and when, a few minutes later, he came upon a water hole with some brush spreading from its edge to the foot of a rocky overhang, he decided it was a good place to make camp. The water hole was in a broad, low-sided ravine at the far end of which the prairie took command of the land again, stretching flat and featureless to the straight line of the horizon behind which the trailing arc of the sun slipped in a blaze of crimson. Then the colour faded and night clamped down.

Jubal combated the dark and cold with the warm glow of a fire. He dug into his dwindling supplies and eked out enough to make three more meals. He had finished eating the first of these and was pouring a second mug of coffee when the wagons rumbled into the ravine. They were still a long way off and he had ample time to put out the fire, saddle his horse and ride away from the campsite before they reached it.

He rode out towards the prairie, found an easy route up on to high ground and doubled back. Then he made a new camp, without benefit of a fire, which looked down into and across the ravine towards the water hole. As he had guessed – for the water was shown on the map Agnew gave him – the train had been heading for the spot. He lay, wrapped in his blanket, watching as the big blond organized night camp, aligning the wagons in a half-circle under the rock overhang with the water hole inside the curving defences. He continued to watch for a while as the men attended to the horses and the

109

women lit fires and prepared a meal. He took particular note of Russ Longstreet, who examined the still warm ash of Jubal's fire, then stood for a long time staring out towards the prairie.

Jubal watched until the exhaustion he had held in check for so long overtook him and his vision blurred. Then he surrendered to the need for sleep: the reason he had abandoned the camp below. An easy sleep, unspoiled by concern that a killer knew his defences were down. But even though he was certain he was safe, his mind would not allow him to forget the Longstreets. And as he slid down into the slough of exhaustion, the voice of Clarke called after him.

'Doc, did you make a mistake. Ain't nothin' ... He must have thought there really was ... For trying to double-cross the boss like that ...' Then Russ's voice exploded: *'Shut up ... Shut up ... Shut up.'*

A dreamless sleep slammed down the shutters on memory. It seemed to last for only seconds before it was shattered by a waking nightmare. But many hours had passed, for the sun was shafting cold, bright yellow light into the ravine. It was not the breaking of day which awoke Jubal and the men and women below him. Sound, not light. The high-pitched, insane war-cries of the Sioux Indians as they swept in to the attack.

They galloped in from the east with the glare of the sun behind them and their whoops announcing terror ahead of them. Two of the white men were already dead, sprawled on the floor of the ravine with knives growing out of their chests. The ghastly scalping scars on their heads told of silent death striking out of the dark: the men killed as they stood guard. Now others died, hit by hissing arrows that thudded into bodies in the process of shaking off sleep.

Rifle and revolver fire cracked and crackled and this first burst of panic shooting sent two braves sprawling from their ponies. The surviving Indians left their mounts voluntarily, leaping to the ground as they burst through the gaps between the parked wagons. Arrows were loosed from twanging bowstrings. Knives rose and plunged. Tomahawks twisted through the air.

It was the same band of Indians which had pursued Jubal and the Longstreets. The renegade Sioux braves exiled by their own tribe and forced into vicious foraging far from their familiar hunting grounds. Jubal recognized their emaciated forms and raddled faces and as he watched them he realized why they had abandoned the fight against three men. Two braves already had rifles and two more possessed revolvers stolen from the dead sentries. Now, as each white man or woman fell to pour life blood on to the ground, a brave leapt forward to snatch up the firearms which clattered from limp hands.

What were three men and their possessions to such a large band of hunters? When there was a heavily laden wagon train close at hand?

A large band, but rapidly getting smaller as the whites retaliated against the dawn attack. The big blond was asserting his command, driving panic out of his people and exhorting them to fight back with disciplined coldness. But the final outcome was inevitable. For every one brave who pitched to the ground with blood gushing from exploded flesh, two or three whites fell.

Jubal watched with horror as the blood-lusting Sioux spread indiscriminate slaughter across the camp. Men, women and even the smallest children were blasted, stabbed or hacked down by shrieking braves whose own heavy losses were caused by insane recklessness. With utter disregard for cover, the Indians raced from one wagon to the next, to leap aboard, slaughter and leap down again. As they sprang up or down and raced between the wagons, they were completely exposed to the fire of the whites.

The noise of the battle amounted to a catalogue of terror. Ceaseless gunfire, men shouting, women screaming, children crying, braves whooping and horses snorting their panic. Then came the roaring of flames as a brave systematically hurled burning kindling on to five wagons before a group of bullets exploded his head. Men, women and children leapt from the burning wagons, clothing and hair aflame. Flying lead or

111

flashing blades ended their agony in blood-gushing death.

And then, as suddenly as it had begun, it was over. A fusillade of shots, a scream and then silence except for the crackle of flames. Even the horses all sensed the end at the same moment and became quiet. The big blond leader of the immigrants appeared at the rear of a wagon, stood in a swaying crouch for a moment, then pitched out on to the ground and remained utterly still. The braves gathered in a group amid the drifting smoke and there were just ten of them left. Two of these were badly wounded and both collapsed as the Indians set to work. Their companions did not offer assistance. They had too many chores to attend to. First recapturing as many ponies as they were able to round up. Then loading the animals with every scrap of food and every weapon they could find amid the havoc and carnage they had created. Finally they undertook the gruesome task of scalping every white head that had not been burned free of hair.

The two wounded braves died before the work was completed and their bodies were left where they had fallen as the survivors rode out, leading the pack ponies behind them. They went eastwards, into the hills and towards the fully-risen sun. Jubal watched them out of sight before he rose and saddled the stallion. As he rode along the side of the ravine, down the slope at the end and then back to the ravaged camp, he tried to analyse his reaction to the slaughter he had witnessed.

But he discovered there was nothing to analyse. On waking to such a nightmare scene he had been gripped by horror. But instead of mounting as he witnessed each new act of revolting violence, the horror had diminished. Until, at the end, he harboured no emotion of any kind. Even as he had watched the scalpings: seen the blood-sodden chunks of flesh clinging to the hair and heard the awesome sound of ripping human skin, he had felt nothing.

So he extended his deliberations, asking himself why he was heading back into the ravine instead of away from it – continuing the trip to Cheyenne that was so important to him. As he neared the devastation spread around the water hole, he told himself he was checking to ensure that no one was left alive and suffering. But he knew he was telling and accepting a lie.

The stallion was reluctant to close in on the water hole, nostrils flaring to the smell of blood and ash. The horses corralled under the rock overhang remained morbidly docile, familiar with the frightening odours. Jubal hitched his mount to the outward-facing rear wheel of an unburned wagon and moved through the defensive line that had proved so ineffective. He felt something now: a churning of nausea in his stomach as the scents which had spooked the stallion were sucked down his throat. The cloying sweetness of burnt flesh was the worst odour, permeating the cold morning air like cheap perfume. And what made the horror harder to take was the fact that most of the seared corpses were either women or children who had been concealed inside the wagons for safety.

But not all. Men had been burned to death as well. Jubal, his stubbled face set in lines that pretended cold indifference to his surroundings, looked into the scorched bed of the canvasless wagon that had led the train. Two boys – about Andy's age, he was forced to conclude – and a woman were sprawled there in blackened death. So, too, was Clarke Longstreet. The straw mattress upon which the injured man had been lying had been set alight by flaming canvas. From the easy, almost relaxed attitude of the charred body, it seemed that Clarke had been consumed by the flames as he lay in merciful unconsciousness. He was naked, of course, his clothes reduced to ash and soot. The dressings on his shoulder and neck wounds had also disintegrated. The scar below his ear and the hole in his shoulder were what made the identification positive. Not enough of his face was left intact to be recognizable.

Jubal turned away from the wagon and began to move among the slumped corpses – red, white and black. He glanced fleetingly at each and with every new shock of sudden death he looked upon, his feeling of nausea lessened. So that when

113

he located the form of Russ Longstreet, Jubal's expression was a true reflection of his emotions. He was in the grip of a cold indifference.

The elder brother was slumped close to the edge of the water hole. Two other bodies hung head first into the sun-dappled water and a third floated at the centre. The water was tinted pink by spilled blood. Longstreet was sprawled on his back and held a seeming two-handed death grip on the shaft of an arrow which had sunk deep into the centre of his stomach.

But he was not yet dead. He held on to a slender thread of life with the same tenacity as he grasped the arrow. But it was a struggle he was destined to lose. Even as Jubal watched, the enormous bloodstain surrounding the arrow expanded and deepened in colour. Fresh blood was pumped out around the wooden shaft with each shallow breath Longstreet took. His hands and face looked milk white beneath the grime, as if the flesh had already been drained dry of blood.

As Jubal stepped in front of the shafting sun to cast a shadow across the dying man, Longstreet flicked open his eyes.

'Not like River's Bend, uh?' he asked, his voice croaking but the words distinct.

Jubal squatted down beside him. 'River's Bend?'

'We all stayed outta that one, Cade. But Clarke and me got caught in the middle here. He's gotta be dead, I guess?'

'Good guess,' Jubal replied.

'Easy for him?'

'Easier than for you.'

'You could help me.' He looked more like his brother than ever now, as an expression of pleading filled his eyes. 'And I don't mean to stay alive. I ain't that stupid.'

'I don't owe you anything,' Jubal told him evenly.

'That can be changed. If I tell you to go open the package Ben Agnew gave you.'

'What does that change?' Jubal wanted to know. 'I know what's inside it.'

114

Incredibly, Longstreet forced a weak grin across his haggard features. 'Like Fairchild reckoned he knew. Go open it, Cade. Then, if you figure I've done you a favour, come back and do me one. Put a bullet in me.'

His eyes flicked away from Jubal's impassive face and he stared up into the sky. Naked terror twisted his features and Jubal thought the man was looking out of life into death. But instead of the death rattle it was a muted shriek of fear that burst from the bloodless lips. Jubal looked over his shoulder and saw the reason for Longstreet's horror. A half-dozen buzzards had swooped down out of the morning sky and were perched on the lip of the ravine. The ugly birds surveyed the scene of slaughter with rapacious eyes.

'Go look, Cade,' Longstreet urged. 'And get back here fast ... Please?'

He spoke the final word as if it came from a foreign language and he was not sure how to pronounce it. Jubal met the terrified gaze for a few moments, then nodded and stood up.

'You'll come back?' Longstreet called after him as Jubal moved away from the sprawled and twisted dead.

Jubal did not reply. The stallion was standing stock-still beside the wagon, ears pricked and eyes wide. Jubal's fingers felt numb as he worked on unfastening the flap of the bulging saddlebag. He did not think it was just because of the cold weather. When he had drawn out the package, he turned it over and over several times in his hands. But it was not a hard decision to make, for Longstreet was in no position to say what he had without good reason. Jubal hesitated only because he felt a cold fear of the implications of the words.

Suddenly, he stooped down to pick up a Sioux arrow. The sharp metal head sliced easily through the string and seals and then he tore frantically with trembling fingers at the wrapping. His eyes blazed, his nostrils flared and his lips formed into a thin, compressed line as the skin was drawn taut over his features. For stretched seconds he stared down at the contents of the package. Then he allowed them to flutter to the ground: a sheaf of blank sheets of paper cut to the shape and size of bank notes.

He whirled, snatching the Spencer from the saddleboot, and lunged into a run back towards the water hole. His boots kicked at and stamped on uncomplaining flesh as he ran in a direct line for his objective. But the haste was futile. He saved a bullet and lost the answers to a thousand questions that screamed silently from the turmoil of his rage. Longstreet's hands were now clasped in a genuine death grip around the shaft of the arrow and there was no longer any breathing to pump blood from the wound.

Jubal's anger was vented in a low groan of anguish. But fresh rage was bred inside him as he whirled and raced back to where the stallion waited. The animal's fear caused him to respond eagerly to the rider's viciously landed heels and he rocketed into a full-stretch gallop towards the rising sun.

The buzzards waited until the sound of the beating hooves had faded. Then, with shrieks of triumph, the birds lifted their evil bodies from the lip of the ravine and zoomed down for their morning meal. At noon, the high sun began to dry the fleshless bones of the dead.

CHAPTER TEN

The Sioux had ridden east from the scene of the slaughter, but Jubal saw nothing of the braves. On the long ride back to St. Louis he saw nothing that he would ever remember. For he travelled in a detached world of his own, breathing out rage and sucking it in again: the environment beyond his being kept at bay by an encircling wall of hate.

He did not recognize the tormented area of the ancient rock fall, littered with the buzzard-stripped skeletons of dead Indians. Nor the abandoned farmstead under the bluff with the maggot-eaten corpse of Fairchild slumped in the yard. As he rode across the spread of Ben Lovell he did not hear the shouted words of the rancher's hands which were hurled at him. Nor did he see the shock of recognition on the faces of the people in River's Bend as he galloped through the tiny town.

He was not aware of resting, sleeping, eating or buying supplies in Kansas City. But when he saw the familiar skyline of St. Louis silhouetted against the horizon ahead of him, he knew he must have done all these things. For neither the stamina of the man himself nor his horse could have been maintained over such a span of time and distance. But until he saw the end of the journey in sight the private world of his existence admitted nothing of material nature. In a fleeting moment of retrospect, the days merged with the nights and the terrain over which he had passed seemed like a grey, featureless wilderness tinged with the red of anger when his rage had boiled to frequent peaks. But some involuntary mental process had warned him to rest and feed himself and his horse: just as it had guided him, without resort to active thinking, along a precise backtrack of his outward journey.

It was nightfall as he emerged from behind the wall of

hate: by the process of drawing this force within himself and extruding the anger that had been tormenting him for so long. This exchange produced both a mental and physical metamorphosis in Jubal. Anger had been blazing hot. Hatred was ice cold. Thus, the frozen quality of Jubal's expression was a truthful mirror of how he felt inside as he dismounted and led the stallion towards the single-storey frame house in which the Agnews lived.

It was eight o'clock and the night was dark with just an occasional star winking through a gap in the cloud cover. The moon was a mere patch of muted blue without shape or substance. Windows at each side of the doorway showed up as solid blocks of yellow spilling their excess light across the front yard.

His movements slow and deliberate, Jubal hitched the stallion, drew the Spencer from its boot and stepped heavily on the stoop. His approach had been heard and he saw a shadow move across the window on his left. But he neither knocked nor waited for the door to be opened. He did not even try the handle to see if the door was locked. He raised his right leg and lashed out, heel forward. His boot connected with the panel just below the handle and the door smashed around on its axis. It crashed into the wall and a picture shook free and hit the floor with a shatter of broken glass.

Gloria Agnew was transfixed in an open doorway halfway along the hall. She wore a more modestly cut gown tonight, and no jewellery. She had been interrupted in the process of brushing her long blonde hair and it gleamed in the lamplight as it fell to her shoulders. The hair framed her once beautiful face which was set in an expression of terror: eyes dragged incredibly wide and lips pulled open in a silent scream. Her small breasts rose and fell rapidly. Her knuckles were white as her hands gripped the hairbrush.

'I want Andy!' Jubal snarled.

He took a step forward and caught sight of himself in a full-length mirror hung on the wall.

He looked ghastly. The stubble of countless days was

formed into a shaggy beard. His flesh and his clothes were caked with mud. The whites of his eyes and his teeth gleamed in unconcealed evil. Then he was beyond the mirror and the woman was driven into movement by terror. Her need to scream forced a pathetic moan from her lips as she backed into the room.

Jubal looked around her and saw luxurious furnishings: deep pile carpets, spindly legged tables and chairs, delicate ornaments. *Doc, did you make a mistake. Ain't nothin' but blank paper in that package Agnew give you.* Jubal supplied the endings to all those remarks Clarke Longstreet had been prevented from completing.

He whirled and opened the door across the hallway. A study, rich and masculine. Smelling of Agnew's cigar smoke. But Agnew wasn't there. *He (Fairchild) must have thought there really was a hundred grand in the bag.*

Another door crashed open under the onslaught of Jubal's boot. Just enough light to make out the shapes in a luxuriously appointed master bedroom. *For trying to double-cross the boss like that ...* Substitute *Mr. Agnew* for *the boss.*

Jubal kicked open another door and saw Andy Prescott. It was a second bedroom, smaller than the master suite and a lamp burned on a low wick. Andy was sitting up in a narrow bed, sightless eyes staring towards the doorway: out of a face that was a young mask of fear. Then, for a few moments as Jubal's empty eyes raked the room, Andy showed bewilderment. The bedroom was, in fact, a nursery, furnished and decorated for a child half Andy's age.

'Jubal!' The boy's face was suddenly filled with joy and there was not a hint of doubt in the shout. He hurled off the bedcovers and leapt from the narrow cot, then raced across the room: familiarity with his surroundings negating his blindness.

Jubal sank into a stoop and held out an arm, sweeping the boy off his feet as he straightened. Andy hugged him around the neck and Jubal tightened his one-armed grip. The boy sensed the man's joyful relief. But he could not, of course, see the frozen expression that revealed a hatred not yet abated.

'Jubal!' Andy said again, softer, and began to sob.

'It's okay, son,' Jubal whispered as he turned away from the nursery.

Despite the conflict of joy and hate, Jubal was aware of Andy's glowing health that told of the comfort and care he had experienced in the house. But this mattered not at all as he strode along the hallway and went into the plush living room. Gloria Agnew was standing in front of a roaring log-fire, pressing the hairbrush against her middle as if she had a bad stomach pain. But it was mental agony that glowed in her staring eyes.

'Where's Agnew?' Jubal rasped, setting the boy down.

Andy, clothed in a freshly laundered nightgown that reached to his ankles, now became conscious of the inner force that was tormenting Jubal.

'We've been good to him,' the woman pleaded. 'Ask him Haven't we been good to you, darling?'

'Yes, ma'am,' Andy replied, his head hanging low.

An oil-painting above the big fireplace caught Jubal's attention and he stared at it for long seconds in the silence that followed the boy's answer. The picture appeared to show Andy when he was half his present age. The same slender frame, unruly blond hair, snub nose and wide eyes. But it could not be a picture of Andy.

'He was our son,' Gloria Agnew explained woefully when she saw what had captured Jubal's attention. 'His name was Curtis. Curtis Agnew. He died when he was five years old. I'm not able to have another child.'

Jubal looked into her face and sensed she was searching his features for a sign of compassion. Jubal did not even try to search himself for pity. He knew none existed.

'So you tried to steal a replacement,' he replied coldly.

'It was as if the Lord sent Andy to me,' she responded.

'You tried to steal Andy and you sent out three hired hands to kill me,' Jubal accused. 'Far out, so you'd be completely safe.'

The woman began to cry, silently. The tears spilled from her eyes and rolled down her wan cheeks, then dripped from her chin to form spots of grey on her white dress. 'I need Andy,' she pleaded softly. 'I can't go on living without him. I can't stay in this house alone unless I keep Andy.' Her voice began to rise, becoming shrill. 'Can you understand what it was like? Trailing after my husband like a dog. Sitting outside waiting while he was at business meetings. Waiting in hotel lobbies while he played poker. Riding behind him when he went out to check the fields and the stock. I've only started to live again since we brought Andy here.'

'I was supposed to die so you could live,' Jubal replied tonelessly. 'And Andy had to give up the chance of regaining his sight. Where's your husband, lady?'

'Right behind you, Cade,' Ben Agnew growled, thrusting a Colt revolver against Jubal's spine. 'You shouldn't have left the stallion outside and the door open.'

Jubal was already tense. The voice of the man he intended to kill and the thud of the gun into his back swayed him forward a fraction and held him there.

'Your double cross didn't work, Agnew,' Jubal said softly.

'My men?'

'Dead.'

'You?'

'Just Fairchild. The Sioux killed the Longstreets.'

'One of them talked,' Agnew growled. 'You haven't had time to get to Cheyenne and back.'

'Russ Longstreet needed a favour,' Jubal replied. 'All he did was tell me to open the package. Guess the man in Cheyenne doesn't exist, uh?'

'The street doesn't exist,' Agnew augmented. 'My wife has told you why?'

'It's a sad story,' Jubal replied. 'But I'm fresh out of sympathy.'

'And money,' Agnew came back. 'That hundred thousand ... I'm willing to give you a package of the real stuff if you'll let us keep the boy.'

'Jubal!' Andy cried, flinging his arms around his guardian's legs.

Caked mud crumbled and dropped to the floor.

'Please?' the woman implored.

'No deal,' Jubal said coldly.

'That's what I thought,' Agnew replied in the same tone. 'Why I never made the offer at first. I've never killed a man in my life. It was cowardly to give the job to others. Now I guess I'll have to —'

'No, Ben!' his wife screamed. 'The boy would never —'

There was a chance that she would be able to talk him out of squeezing the trigger of the revolver. But Jubal had learned the hard way not to rely on the actions or trust the words of others. In the kind of world that had become his, a man survived by a mixture of two brands of good fortune – that which fate bestowed upon him and that which he made himself.

He whirled around, as Agnew was distracted by his wife's pleading words. In whirling, he also sank into a crouch and lashed out with his right leg. The woman and Andy screamed simultaneously. Gloria Agnew did not move, but the boy was hurled hard to the floor. The shock of the abrupt action jolted a reflex from Agnew and the Colt exploded. The bullet ploughed a furrow across the back of Jubal's coat and the material was not sufficient to deflect its course. It spun straight into the woman's stomach just above where she clutched the hairbrush to her. She screamed again as the impact of the lead in her flesh drove her backwards, doubling her up as she tripped and fell into the fire. Her scream changed note from shock to agony as the flames took hold of her gown and seared furiously around her writhing body.

Jubal completed his whirl, swinging the Spencer. The stock missed Agnew's head by the merest fraction as he charged forward. Jubal was unbalanced and struggled to remain upright: to be ready for a counter-attack. But Agnew's action was not to avoid the blow. Instead, he sprinted towards the flaming body of his wife. Jubal righted himself and saw what was happening. He saw that the woman's body was now

122

still and that Agnew had hurled away the Colt. There was no longer any screaming. Just the frightened sobbing of Andy.

Jubal dragged his cold gaze away from the horrendous tableau of Agnew hauling the body of his wife from the fire and beating at the flaming gown with his bare hands. He saw Andy curled up on the floor, the slight form trembling. He went to him, scooped him up in a single arm hold and rested the Spencer barrel across the back of a chair, aimed at Agnew. Andy continued to shake, but his sobbing ceased.

'She's dead, Agnew,' Jubal pronounced.

The words drove the man to a more frantic beating at the flames and he was not still until the last flicker was out and he was crushing the unfeeling head of his wife to his chest. Then he looked across at Jubal holding the boy in one arm and the rifle in the other.

He was the same man dressed in the same way as when Jubal had first seen him. But now he looked many years older and seemed shrivelled up. Every trace of arrogant self-assurance and dignity had evaporated. His eyes were blurred by tears.

'It should have been me,' he moaned. 'I'm the one who ...' He couldn't go on.

'Her suffering's over,' Jubal replied tonelessly. 'You're the one who'll live with the regrets.'

Jubal realized he had changed his mind. It was an involuntary decision: his mind working without volition in the same way it had on the long ride back. Every inch of the way, he had been intent upon killing Agnew. But not any more. Looking at the hollow shell of the man, Jubal could almost feel pity for him. For he had held Mary to him in such a way a few moments after her death. But he rejected pity and instead felt a sense of elation at the punishment Agnew was destined to suffer. And Jubal had good reason to know the harshness of this brand of punishment.

'I didn't get to Cheyenne, Agnew,' he said. 'But in my book, I reckon you owe me the five thousand.'

'Let's go, Jubal,' Andy whispered hoarsely. 'Pa used to

say a man ought to quit when he's ahead.'

'Sorry, son,' Jubal told the boy. 'But if I don't collect, I'm not ahead.' He lightened his tone. 'And you don't get into the clinic.'

Agnew gently rested his wife's blackened head on the rug and stood up. 'I owe it to the boy,' he said softly. 'At least he gave Gloria some happiness in the final few days of her life.'

He crossed the room, a broken man, and went out into the hallway. Jubal set down Andy and led him after Agnew. They went into the leather- and cigar-smelling study and Jubal watched coldly as Agnew opened a safe and drew out a stack of bills. They were all hundred dollar notes and it did not take long to count off the five grand demanded by Jubal. Agnew closed the safe, put the money on the front of the desk and sat down behind it. His shoulders seemed to jut up to flank his face, as if he had no neck. Jubal advanced farther into the room and picked up the money. He continued to level the Spencer in the one-handed grip, so had to release Andy so that he could pick up the money and thrust it into his pocket. Then he backed over to the doorway, leading Andy again. He didn't trust Agnew. Although the old man seemed physically limp: drained of the will to do more than hold himself partially upright in the leather chair, there was a certain strength of purpose in his misted eyes.

'The boy will be safe in the clinic,' Agnew said softly when Jubal and Andy reached the doorway. 'I give you my word on that.'

Jubal didn't reply for several seconds, sensing the sightless eyes staring up at him from out of the pale face below. Then he nodded: 'I believe that.'

'But you I intend to kill, Cade. It was my hand on the gun, but that don't make any difference. If you hadn't come back, Gloria would still be alive and happy. I won't be content until I've killed the man responsible for her death.'

Jubal nodded again, more emphatically this time. There was the merest hint of sadness in his otherwise cold eyes as he replied. 'I know how you feel,' he said softly.